Claiming What's Mine

— *The Sexy Simmons Series*—

Angie Daniels

D0062499

Caramel Kisses
Publishing

ISBN-13: 978-1-941342-09-1

Caramel Kisses
Publishing

Caramel Kisses Publishing
PO Box 2313
Chesterfield, VA 23832
www.caramelkissespublishing.com

Claiming What's Mine

— *The Sexy Simmons Series* —

Angie Daniels

Caramel Kisses
Publishing

DEDICATION

To all of my loyal readers who've been
begging for more, this book is for you!

Chapter One

Jennifer Simmons and her husband Shaun were headed toward the register when she snapped her fingers. "Sweetheart, I forgot barbecue sauce."

He smiled down at his wife's adorable face. "Why don't you go ahead and get in line while I get it?"

Nodding, she tilted her chin and met Shaun's lips as he pressed them against hers in a sweet kiss. "I'll be right back."

He turned, headed down the grocery store aisle, scanning the shelves for the right sauce for his wife's amazing ribs that she slow-cooked until they were practically falling off the bones. His chest swelled with pride.

He was a lucky man.

After he'd lost his wife to an aneurism, leaving him to raise three small kids on his own, he'd never thought he'd have a second chance at love. And then he met Jennifer during a fender-bender and it had been the best nine years of his life.

His children now had lives of their own. His daughter Sheyna was married to Jace Beaumont and they were the parents of his only grandchild Jace Jr.

Scott had recently married his beautiful fiancée Zanaa. And his son Darnell ... Well, he wasn't quite sure what he was doing except partying and dating as many women as he could fit on his calendar. Hopefully, he would soon be ready to settle down.

Shaun found the condiments and was heading down the aisle when he spotted a little kid running in his direction.

"Chance, come back here!"

He noticed a woman hurrying down the aisle as she pushed a shopping cart, and before the little boy had an opportunity to rush past him, Shaun reached down and scooped him in his arms.

"Whoa! Slow down little tyke," he said, causing the little boy to start laughing hysterically. Smiling, Shaun swung him around and the second he saw his face the air rushed from his lungs. Mahogany skin, large amber eyes and a purple birthmark right behind his left ear. He stared in disbelief.

Was it possible?

"Thank you so much for catching him," the woman began, drawing his attention. "I should have known the second I let him out of the cart he would start running around the store."

Shaun looked at the beautiful woman with butter-colored skin, brown eyes and wild, curly brown hair.

"Boys are always a handful."

"I'm starting to figure that out." She laughed, and the little boy practically dove into her arms. Even after Shaun had released him, he couldn't stop staring at him.

"I'm Liberty Roth and this here is Chance."

Reaching up, Shaun ruffled the little boy's curls. "It's a pleasure meeting you both." He dropped his hand and released a nervous laugh. "Forgive me..., but can I ask who his father is?"

Her eyes widened. "Excuse me?"

"I'm sorry, but—"

"Shaun! There you are..." his wife said, interrupting. He swung around to spot Jennifer coming up the aisle with their cart. "I forgot to get cheese and lettuce for tacos tonight." She drew close to him, stopped and must have noticed the disturbed look on his face because her eyes traveled from him to Liberty.

"Hello," she said and held out her hand. "I'm Jennifer and you are...?"

The beauty smiled. "I'm Liberty and this is Chance."

"It's a pleasure to meet..." Shaun realized the exact moment his wife looked at the little boy and realization sank in. "Oh my goodness! He looks just like Dee."

Shaun nodded and was relieved his wife agreed. "I was getting ready to say the same thing."

Liberty looked at the both of them, confused. "Who's Dee?"

"My son, Darnell. That's his son, isn't it?"

She shook her head. "I don't know anyone named Darnell." She lowered Chance back into the cart then glanced down at the watch on her slender wrist. "I better go. Thanks again for catching him for me. It was a pleasure meeting both of you. Chance, say goodbye."

"Bye!" he cried then gave a goofy laugh and a familiar smile that caused Shaun's stomach to clench. He knew that look anywhere. It had once belonged to his wife.

Liberty gave a quick wave, then turned and pushed her cart down the aisle.

"You know she lying, right?" Jennifer replied.

Shaun nodded. "Yep. I don't care what she says. That little boy is my grandson."

♥ ♥ ♥

"I'll also have a slice of peach pie," Sheyna Beaumont said, completing her order and handed the waitress her menu.

"Sounds good. I'll be back shortly with your iced tea."

As soon as the perky young waitress left to help customers seated at another table, Sheyna gazed over at her sister-in-law and grinned as she said, "You think Jaden suspects anything?"

Danica Beaumont gave her a saucy grin as she brushed a long, reddish brown curl from her face. "He doesn't have a clue. I want our anniversary to be a weekend he'll never forget."

"A weekend in Bermuda. Trust me, he'll never suspect a thing."

Smiling, she released a heavy sigh. "I hope so. Although, I feel a little guilty planning a romantic weekend just to try and get my way."

"Why not? There is nothing wrong with a woman using what she's got to get what she wants," Sheyna told her, shaking her brown curls with an amused grin.

"We're being bad!" Danica said with a laugh, then she tilted her head to one side, considering the possibility with a nervous smile. "You and I both know I gave up modeling to move to Sheraton Beach. I don't think Jaden is going to like my decision to model again."

Sheyna ignored the uncertainty in her voice. "But it's not like you're going back to hitting the runway. You're just promoting your swimsuit design. Just tell him you're on your way to being the next Kimora Lee Simmons."

The tall beauty folded her arms across her breasts.

Danica didn't look convinced.

The waitress returned with their drinks. Sheyna heard her phone ringing. She scooped up her red Dooney bag, dug in the side pocket and glanced down at the number across the screen. It was her father. She signaled to Danica she was stepping out, and then rose from her chair. "Hey Daddy," she said merrily as she sauntered out of the dining room and into the hall.

"Hello sweetheart. How's everyone doing?"

"We're good. Don't forget JJ has a soccer game on Wednesday," she quickly reminded.

"Don't worry. You tell him his grandpa wouldn't miss it for the world."

She loved her father. He had been an amazing provider and adored his only grandson. Sheyna wandered over to a window and stared out at the ocean. Boats were docked all along the harbor. "What's going on Daddy?" They usually talked at least once or twice a week, but they had just spoken last night.

"I was trying to find Darnell and was wondering if you knew where he was?"

She gave a rude snort. "Probably with some chick." Her youngest brother had a reputation of being a heartbreaker. She wasn't sure if he'd ever settle down despite several attempts at fixing him up. "Have you tried Scott?"

"He wasn't home when I called." She didn't miss the frustration in his voice.

"Daddy, what's wrong?"

There was a slight hesitation. "This may sound crazy but I just ran into a woman at the grocery store with a little boy who looked just like Dee."

"What?" she gasped.

"Sheyna, it's true!" she heard Jennifer yelling into the phone.

"How... what...?" She took a deep breath and started again. "Was it one of his exes?" *And if so, which one?* There had been so many, she gave up trying to keep up years ago.

"She denies even knowing him, but a father knows his genes and *that* boy is my grandson. I'd bet my entire pension check on it."

"Wow! You're serious." Sheyna racked her brain trying to remember if there was anyone who stood out. "How old's the little boy? Do you know the woman's name?"

"The little boy... his name is Chance, looks to be around four, and his mother's name is Liberty Roth."

"Liberty Roth," she mumbled repeatedly under her breath hoping that it sounded familiar, but it didn't ring a bell. "The name doesn't sound familiar."

"My son has a lot of explaining to do. You know how I feel about men taking care of their responsibilities," he said, and there was no mistaking the disappointment.

"Daddy, I'm sure Dee has a good explanation. In fact, maybe he doesn't even know he has a child." *Until I found out otherwise, I was going to try and give him the benefit of a doubt.*

"I sure hope so," he said and then sighed. "Well, if you get in touch with your brother have him call me."

"I will Daddy. I'll call you tomorrow."

Sheyna ended the call, her brain racing with possibilities. Was it possible? She had a nephew to spoil. Jace had several nieces and nephews that they adored, but this little boy was possibly a Simmons. And that made it worth finding out.

♥ ♥ ♥

"Welcome home."

Scott Simmons stepped into the large master bedroom to find his beautiful wife lying seductively across the bed in a short, red nightie.

"Damn, babe. What's going on?"

"I decided to take off work early so I could greet my handsome husband home," she purred. Those large golden eyes were burning with fire and caused his skin to suddenly overheat.

"Is that so?"

Zanaa nodded. "Yes, now come over here and kiss your horny wife."

She didn't have to tell him twice. Scott walked across the room and dove over onto the bed beside her, causing her to erupt in a fit of laughter. "Now what was it you wanted to talk about?" he murmured before pressing his lips against hers and kissing her with so much love and devotion. Every time he laid eyes on his wife, he had to draw a deep breath and remember how lucky he was to have found Zanaa.

When Scott had moved into La Chateau Condominiums, in the unit beside her, he had no idea he would not only end up in his neighbor's bed but that the two would also fake an engagement for her family that ended in them discovering the greatest love of all.

"How was the conference?" Zanaa managed between kisses.

He leaned on one elbow, looking down at her smooth, brown face as he spoke. "The conference was brutal. Three days away from my wife is too long. I showed them the demo for the game, waited on a stamp of approval, and then hopped on the first plane back."

Lying flat on her back, she gazed up at him and frowned. "If that's the case, you could have just sent the demo electronically."

His brow rose. "And risk a hacker stealing my game before its release. No way."

She giggled and shook her head. "No we definitely couldn't have that."

His fingers slid across the nightie, traveling slowly over the soft satin material and when he reached the hem, Scott slipped under and discovered she wasn't wearing any panties. "Looks like someone shaved."

"I got a Brazilian wax," she replied in a strained voice just as Scoot dipped one finger between her folds and into her warm center. With a groan, she lifted her hips off the bed, meeting his touch.

"Don't you have a wedding tomorrow?"

The wedding coordinator nodded and he saw the desperate need burning in her eyes as she whispered, "I do but Ashley is handling all the last minute details."

Scott agreed. "Remind me to put a little something extra in her Christmas stocking this year."

Her assistant was quite capable of handling just about anything which allowed plenty of opportunities for the newlyweds to steal away. They had been married two years. Since then the couple had built a spacious five-bedroom house in Wilmington, Delaware with the hope of filling it with children of their own.

"I sure will," Zanaa moaned while rocking her hips to the rhythm of his finger. "Now quit talking."

"Ooh, bossy! I like that," he teased as he watched her eyes as she writhed beneath his touch. His thumb caressed her clit until his wife's breath became strangled and desperate. "I think someone missed me. Am I right?"

She hissed in a breath and closed her eyes. "Yes, sweetheart, I missed you. Now please... I need you inside me."

Scott heard the need in her voice as he lowered the spaghetti straps until her breasts were exposed. Then he dipped his head and took one of her chocolate nipples into his mouth, licking and sucking until she was whimpering his name in a broken voice. Her hands traveled desperately up and down his arms until she grabbed ahold of his head, drew him back until his gaze met hers and whispered, "I said I need you now."

"Whatever my wife wants, she shall get," he murmured and kissed her once more before shifting off the bed. While removing his clothes Scott stared down at her lying there, legs spread wide, wanting and waiting. "I need a picture of you just like that to get me through those long nights when I'm away from you."

Zanaa giggled. "How about later we do our own private photo session?"

That signature Simmons smile curved his mouth while he slipped off his slacks. "Can I set up the tripod?"

"Absolutely," she cooed and Scott watched the way her eyes widened with anticipation as he lowered his boxers to the carpet and kicked them away.

Naked, he crawled back across the bed then his lips and tongue were moving over her flesh with deliberate yet slow strokes. By the time he'd reached the tender flesh between her thighs, Zanaa was practically in tears. His tongue pushed her higher and higher, licking and sucking until she had finally reached her peak.

"Scott, now!" she cried.

He shifted between her parted thighs then caught her gaze as he drove long and hard into her waiting body. Zanaa gasped and arched her hips taking him deeper.

"Shit!" Scott moaned. "Hold up... otherwise this is going to be over way too soon," he managed in a strained voice.

Zanaa smiled and dragged his face to hers for a long kiss. "I'm not worried. We got all night."

"I like the sound of that." He kissed her while his hips rocked, setting a rhythm that his wife followed. Just as he expected, within minutes he felt his body spiraling completely out of control. Scott looked down into her eyes as her walls clenched and she held him tightly.

"I'm about to come," she whispered as he felt her come apart underneath him.

"So am I..." he mumbled. "So am I." And then his body shattered.

♥ ♥ ♥

Hours later, Scott heard his cell phone ringing. He preferred to ignore it, only he identified the ringtone belonging to one of his family members. Slowly, he slid out from beneath Zanaa's sleeping body, padded over to his jeans and removed the phone from his pocket.

"Hey Sis," he said softly as he stepped out the bedroom not to disturb Zanaa. The night was still young, and she was going to need her rest.

"Hey Scott. How was the meeting?" Sheyna asked.

He moved down the stairs, heading toward the kitchen as he spoke. "My agent was able to sell another design."

"That's wonderful! My big brother the video game mogul." The pride he heard in his little sister's voice caused him to smile.

"Hey, I'm tryna be like the Beaumonts when I grow up," Scott teased.

"Yeah right," she laughed.

By the time he'd started college, Scott had produced his first published video game. It was during his senior year Scott developed a computer game series that had such an enormous following, he'd partnered with Destination Games, and the rest was history. Now he was one of the top developers in the world.

Scott stepped into the large kitchen. Henric, his furry white Husky, was curled up in the corner on his bed, snoring. "What's up with you?"

"Dad and I are looking for Darnell."

"Dee's been working on some big divorce case. Why? What's up?" he asked while opening the refrigerator, and his eyes lit up when he spotted a box of fried chicken.

Sheyna released a heavy sigh as she said, "I think he has a baby mama."

He sputtered with laughter. "Dee? Nah… he would have told me."

"Well Dad says he does." Scott nibbled on a chicken leg while he listened as Sheyna shared what their father had told her.

"What? A little boy?" Scott chuckled loudly between chews. "I wish I could have been there to see that."

"So do I."

"Liberty Roth, huh?" While he leaned back against the marble countertop he pondered the name for a moment. "I've never heard him talk about her but I'm going to definitely have a talk with Lil bro."

"That's if you get to him before I do," she hissed, and was clearly frustrated.

They chatted a few moments more, then Scott ended the call. *Darnell with a son?* This he definitely had to see. His brother was two years younger and thought he was God's gift to women. At one point, the two brothers were considered by their friends as the heartbreakers, moving through towns leaving lines of broken hearts behind. But that was before he'd met Zanaa.

Tomorrow, he would track Darnell down, but right now he'd rather get back in bed with his wife. Naptime was over.

Chapter Two

Darnell slowly raised the slender arm draped across his chest and slid out from beneath it. The entire time his eyes were glued to the golden beauty snoring softly beside him. Was her name Kayla? Or did she say Karen? He scowled.

Dee, man, you're getting too old for this shit.

He rose from the bed and gently lowered her arm over the spot he had just vacated, then pressed a hand to his temple. Last night he'd been out celebrating winning the biggest divorce case of his legal career. A Washington D.C. politician had been hiding millions from his wife, and Darnell with the help of his team, not only uncovered every red cent, but found out he had a pregnant mistress.

He reached down for his slacks and slipped in one leg followed by the other, then reached inside his pocket and stared down at his cell phone. A frown marred his dark forehead as he noticed the numerous missed calls from his father and Sheyna. Even Scott had tried calling him this morning. A feeling of uneasiness settled in. He prayed that nothing was wrong with his father. With high blood pressure, his health wasn't always the best.

Quickly, he worked to get dressed.

"Leaving so soon?"

While buttoning his expensive shirt, Darnell smiled over at the almond-colored beauty who was peering up at him through somber brown eyes. "Yeah sexy. I gotta be in court in a few hours."

"That's too bad," she purred and tossed the covers away. Naked, she did a full-body stretch and her nipples stood up perfectly. "I was hoping for another round of celebrating." She spread her legs, putting her shaved pussy on full display.

Darnell licked his lips and contemplated shedding his clothes and sinking himself deep inside something warm and wet again, but the numerous missed calls from his family were cock-blocking his libido.

"Sorry sweetheart. I'm going to have to take a rain check."

She gave a cute pout. "You promise?"

"Absolutely," he lied, and hurried to finish getting dressed. The sex had been good but he remembered the beauty saying something about being ready to settle down and start a family. Two things he wasn't interested in. He'd tried a few times to have a relationship, and of course his sister Sheyna had been trying to get him to settle down for years. He had even tried talking himself into it. If there was one thing Darnell was good at, it was talking. He had been born with the gift of gab which made him one of the best attorneys in the region. Unfortunately, love and marriage just wasn't in the cards for him.

As he headed to the door, he spotted a diploma from Hampton University on the wall that confirmed her name was Karine. She sauntered her naked, shapely body to the front door then wrapped her arms around his neck, crushing her huge breasts against his chest as she kissed him with enough passion to cause his body to heat and stir.

"I'll call you," he murmured while untangling her arms.

She drew back and brought a slender hand to her waist. "Really? You don't even have my number."

Damn. Darnell released a chuckle, then slid his tongue across his bottom lip the way he knew the women loved. He whipped out his phone and within minutes had her number programmed in and was out the door, strutting down the walk to his Range Rover. Before he even backed out the driveway he hit up Sheyna at her office.

"It's about time!" she barked into the receiver and immediately he wished he had called his brother Scott instead.

"What? Is something wrong with Dad?"

She gasped. "Daddy? Of course not. Why you think that?"

"Because everyone has been blowing up my phone." He realized he was now yelling.

"Relax, Dee...there's nothing wrong. Dad just saw something that has him concerned and he asked me and Scott to track you down."

He pressed a fingertip to his temple again. Why was talking to Sheyna this morning like pulling teeth? "What's going on?"

"Well..," she began and he realized she was talking between sips, probably that foo-foo coffee she liked to drink.

"Well what?" he insisted impatiently.

"Dad said while he was at the grocery store he ran into your baby mama."

Startled, he had to slam on his brakes to keep from hitting the Mini Cooper in front of him. Not a smart move for a lawyer to be sued.

"Baby Mama?" Darnell erupted with a combination of relief and laughter. He had dreaded something far worse. "I'd have to have kids to have a baby's mama."

19

And no matter how much he loved sex, he always strapped up.

"Well according to Dad he ran into a woman by the name of Liberty Roth with a little boy who looks just like you."

Liberty? Liberty Roth? As he maneuvered down Interstate 95 heading toward Sheraton Beach, Delaware, Darnell let the name roll around in his head.

"I don't know a Liberty Roth," he retorted. But then he hadn't remembered the name of the woman he'd slept with last night, therefore, what were the chances of him remembering the name of a woman he'd slept with more than nine months ago?

"Did Dad think to ask this woman if she even knew me?"

"He did ask."

"And?" he asked growing increasingly impatient.

Sheyna breathed a heavy sigh. "And she said she didn't know you."

"Then there you have it," Darnell retorted and punched the steering wheel.

"I told Daddy the same thing but he was adamant. You should have heard him Dee because then you would believe him too." She sucked her teeth. "I knew JJ was Jace's the second I laid eyes on him."

He had to admit that his nephew was the spitting image of his father. With all those Beaumont qualities he could have picked him out in a crowd. "Sheyna, you and Jace are married. It's not the same thing."

"I'm just saying," she replied with attitude. The last thing he wanted was to piss his little sister off.

"Listen Shey-Shey. Trust me. I would know if I had a child," he said with confidence. Using her pet name always made her smile.

"Dad said the little boy has the same birthmark

behind his left ear as you."

Darnell mumbled under his breath. Sheyna had purposely saved that bit of information until the end. He could argue a lot of things, but the purple birthmark there was no denying that. Could it be possible? he pondered. Up until a year ago he spent all of his free time partying, drinking, and hanging out at strip clubs. Had he slipped up in one of his drunken stupors and fathered a child? Darnell scowled. He hoped not. But if he had, why hadn't the mother come to him? He was smart enough to know that accidents happened and condoms weren't a hundred percent, even though he relied heavily on them. But one thing he'd never do was avoid his responsibilities. If there was a child out there with Simmons blood running through his veins, then he wanted to know, although it was highly unlikely. One thing about Darnell "Dee" Simmons, he was careful.

"Darnell, are you listening?" Sheyna said, ripping into his thoughts.

"Yeah, Shey-Shey I'm listening."

"You need to call Daddy because he's really concerned he has a grandson running around that's not a part of his life."

He groaned. "Yeah, I'll call him."

"Okay," she replied with a breath of relief and then there was a slight pause. "Dee… is there any chance he might be your son?"

Darnell suddenly didn't feel quite so confident. "I don't know, but I'm sure the hell going to find out."

$$\Omega \; \Omega \; \Omega$$

"Kick… now punch. Again! Kick…and punch. Other side!"

Liberty led the class through her power pump class

with music pounding out of the iPod docked on the speaker in the corner. "You can do it... you can do it... don't give up! Now lift that leg up and kick... now the other leg."

Liberty instructed her class through the entire forty-five minute workout session, followed by a five-minute stretch that ended right at the end of the song. "That's it for the evening." Liberty managed between breaths, then waved and disconnected the small microphone. "Thank you and see you again on Friday!" The class joined her in a roar of applause. After three workout routines in one day, she was ready for a hot shower, a hot meal and then she was crashing the rest of the evening on the couch.

She was packing her iPod into her duffel bag when Cash came dancing over to her.

"Great class tonight, Liberty." If I keep this up I might shed this baby fat after all."

With a smirk, Liberty lifted her head and stared at her best friend of ten years who was thick, shapely, and completely proud of her body. "What baby? You don't even have a dog," she teased.

Laughing, Cash gave a dismissive wave. "It doesn't matter, I still need to tone up these thunder-thighs before the summer rolls around again."

"Whatever girl." Cash was voluptuous with curves in all the right places. With platinum blond hair cut close to her head, wide eyes, and high cheekbones on a caramel-colored face, she was as beautiful on the outside as she was on the inside. As usual she was wearing big hoop earrings, a Philadelphia Eagles sweatshirt and black leggings.

Laughing, the two cleared the equipment from the platform while the room emptied, then filled up for Zumba class. The gorgeous Dominican sauntered in with enough energy to make Liberty tired from just watching.

"Hola chicas!" she said merrily.

"Hola Amelia. It's all yours." She swung her bag onto her shoulder, then followed Cash out of the eight-hundred square foot studio onto the equipment floor.

"So I'm dying to hear how your coffee date went?"

Liberty slanted her best friend a look. "It was a meet-and-greet. And let's just say it was worth the drive for my favorite caramel macchiato."

Her brow rose. "It was that bad?"

"It was worse," she groaned. "The picture he'd had posted on-line had to have been ten years ago. Drew had a gut and a receding hairline." By the time they had made it outside in the parking lot out front, they were both doubled over with laughter. "Girl, I'm desperate but I'm not that desperate."

Smiling, Cash sent her a sidelong glance. "Then what was wrong with Lee? He's handsome and you said you liked him."

"Yeah, like I like a cousin." Liberty had also met him online. He was an optometrist and a wonderful conversationalist, but there had been no chemistry. One kiss told her everything she needed to know about the future of their relationship. No tingles. No stars.

She liked an attractive man as much as the next woman, but she didn't get all hot and bothered over them. And the rate she was going, she probably never would ever again. Not that it really mattered. Part of her just wasn't interested in falling in love again, instead she focused all her time and energy at work or with her son Chance. But at times she yearned to have someone special in her life.

Liberty pulled the collar up around her bomber jacket. The temperature had dropped considerably in the last several hours and snow was in the forecast. "I think I'm going to take a break from dating until after the holiday season."

They neared Cash's cute yellow VW Bug where she stopped, turned and made a face at her. "Why are you so picky?"

"I'm not picky," Liberty argued as Cash popped the trunk and tossed her gym bag inside. "I just want what I want."

"But what is that?" Cash asked with a roll of the eyes.

Liberty had to pause at that one. "I'll know when I find him," she replied, even though she was starting to think she'd never find a man who met all her qualifications. She didn't feel like she was asking for much. A gorgeous man with an outgoing personality, a great communicator, who liked kids. It wasn't much and yet why couldn't she find that?

"You need to lower your standards a little. Two out of three wants ain't bad."

Liberty glared at her. "This is coming from a woman who only dates men who drive luxury cars and have six-figure salaries."

Cash chuckled, then sobered. "We're not talking about me. I just want Chance to have a father."

"He has a mother," she reminded for the umpteenth time.

Cash held up one hand. "Yes, he does and a great one at that. But a woman can't teach a boy how to be a man."

She couldn't argue that. She had been raised without a mother and her father hadn't known the first thing about training bras and PMS.

Liberty hit her remote starter for her Hyundai Santa Fe, then peered down at her friend. They had attended college together and planned on taking over the world. Instead, Cash moved to Sheraton Beach, Delaware after landing a position as a pediatric nurse. She had eventually convinced Liberty to relocate to the small beach town. And Liberty had opened the hottest fitness center in the area.

Cash clicked the remote starting her vehicle that purred softly like a kitten, then leaned back against the door.

"What are you going to do? Chance keeps asking about his father."

"I don't know. I guess telling him I don't know who he is won't score many points, huh?" she said and tried to make a joke out of it but she knew Cash had a point.

"He needs a father Lib, and you need a good man."

"Fine," Liberty finally said with a sigh. "I'll try dating again after the holidays, I promise. In the meantime, I'll go on another date with Lee."

Cash nodded. "I think that's a good idea. He's a good man, and he adores Chance."

Maybe she was right. Maybe she needed to give up the fantasy of heart palpitations and creaming panties, and settle for loyalty and companionship instead.

"I better go home before I'm late again," she groaned. As an owner and instructor there was free daycare at her gym, but that meant leaving him in the care of one of her childcare assistants for three hours. Instead Chance spent the evenings she had classes at home with the sweet elderly woman who lived two doors down. By the time she arrived home, Chance had already eaten, bathed, and was ready to go home to bed.

Liberty waved, then hopped in her SUV and peeled out the parking lot heading toward Hampton Woods, to the cookie-cutter neighborhood she had called home for the last two years. As she drove, she couldn't help but wonder if maybe Cash was right. Chance needed a positive male role model in his life. Something she'd never had.

After her mother had died, her father spent the rest of his life grieving, and never did allow himself to get close and love his daughter the way a father should. Liberty believed part of it was because she looked so much like her mother and was a constant reminder of the woman he had lost while giving birth to her. He provided a roof over Liberty's head, clothes and food in her stomach but that's where the nurturing ended. She had been an honor student, a math whiz, and a swimming champ, but even being on the front page of the sports section of the *Magnolia Times* newspaper hadn't warranted a pat on the back or an "I'm proud of you." By the time she had turned eighteen, Liberty realized there was nothing she could do about her relationship with her father. She went off to college and started a new life that he had no interest in being a part of. Before Chance had turned one, she had gotten word from a distant cousin, her father had fallen asleep behind the wheel of his truck and had run off the road and was pronounced dead at the scene. She had attended the funeral, needing to see his face one last time so she could have the opportunity to tell him all the great things he had been missing in her life. And then she said goodbye.

Despite their estranged relationship, Liberty had taken his death hard. And as much as she wanted to pretend her father no long mattered, even from his grave, a part of her still craved — with the yearning of a little girl — his approval.

♥ ♥ ♥

Chance came racing into his bedroom as naked as the day she'd brought him into the world. "Mommy can I watch TV?" Chance said and batted his incredibly thick lashes. He was such a ham. How could she resist?

"One hour, then it's lights out," she told him. "Now come here so I can help you get dressed." Chance had insisted on waiting until she had come home so that he could splash around in her jetted garden-size tub. There was probably water all over her bathroom floor from him splashing around, but listening to his infectious laughter made it so worth the mess she was going to have to mop up.

Liberty helped him into a pair of footed Spiderman pajamas, then followed him down the hall. By the time she stepped into his bedroom, Chance already had the television on. She shook her head. That boy knew how to use the remote better than she did.

A few moments later, he was cozy under the warm blankets watching a recorded episode of *Sid the Scientist Kid* while she padded back to her master suite. Liberty stepped into the adjoining bathroom and removed the toy boats from the water and smiled.

If only his father could see him.

Being a single parent wasn't easy and having a little boy sometimes made it even harder. While she cleaned the bathroom, she allowed her mind to flood with warm memories of her beloved husband.

He was considerably older, but age was never an issue. Greg was young at heart and such a lovely man. She remembered being on campus at the University of Illinois at Urbana and stopping Greg to ask for directions to class, only to find out he was her instructor. She spent the entire semester admiring her instructor from afar and since he was considerably older than her, Liberty had no idea Greg had been attracted to her as well. He had waited until grades had been posted for the semester before he asked her out for coffee. They spent the rest of the evening sitting and laughing, and by the time he'd walked her back to her apartment she shared with Cash, they were holding hands and planning a picnic over the weekend. They dated almost a year before he finally proposed. They married in a small ceremony with his family filling the church, although most of them disapproved of him marrying a woman fifteen years younger. The couple had been so happy they were oblivious to everyone's feelings, and were anxious to start a family of their own.

It was another two years before Liberty found out she was pregnant and she decided to wait until her husband's birthday to share the news. That morning Greg was out doing his regular Saturday morning jog through the park when he collapsed on the sidewalk and died instantly of a massive heart attack at forty.

He never knew about Chance.

For weeks, Liberty had walked around in a daze. His parents never cared much for her and insisted on flying the body back to New Hampshire to be buried. Liberty was too numb to argue. She traveled up with his casket, said her private goodbyes to her husband, and then returned to their empty home alone.

It was Cash who insisted she eat and find the strength to pick herself up for the baby's sake. It had been hard, but with every passing day it got easier, and once she felt Chance moving inside, reality had hit her.

She was going to finally have a baby.

Greg's life insurance helped a great deal. She relocated to Sheraton Beach and opened *24/7 Fitness*.

She taught a few evening classes a week, but for the most part, as the owner, Liberty handled the day-to-day operations. That way her evenings were free to spend with Chance. Her son was her pride and joy. She never knew she could love someone that much until she gave birth to him. Cash had been right there beside her.

Liberty carried the wet towels down the hall to the laundry room, tossed them inside, and started the washer. She then walked back to the front of her Cape Cod, into the living room and paused to admire her holiday handiwork. A six-foot tall Douglas fir. It was an annual tradition that the day after Thanksgiving she put up a real tree. Ever since Chance was old enough, the two of them spent Black Friday making Christmas decorations with his art supplies, and then strung popcorn and lights.

It was a labor of love.

As her eyes traveled to the blinking lights, the holiday decorations on the fireplace mantel, and all the other Christmas decors she had bought to brighten up the room, she smiled. Christmas was her favorite time of the season. Under the tree were several presents she had taken her time wrapping long after Chance had gone to sleep. He still believed in Santa so there would be several surprises on Christmas morning, however, she always wanted him to get something wrapped that he knew had come from his mother. Since she had little to no family, the holiday had always just been about the two of them.

Liberty moved over to the couch and wrapped the small fleece blanket around her feet as she lay there daydreaming about a holiday filled with family. While Greg was alive, they did everything to make Christmas special. Sometimes they visited his parents and other times they just rang in the new year together. That was one thing she missed, sharing the holidays with someone special. She loved her son and Cash always tried to find a way to include her, but neither filled the void of having a special man in her life. Liberty sighed. She would love to someday meet someone to share their life with, but she wasn't settling for just anyone.

Chapter Three

It took Darnell one week to find her.

Liberty Roth from Belleville, Illinois had moved to Sheraton Beach three years ago and was the owner of the hottest fitness club on the beach.

She's was also the mother of his son.

Darnell reached down for the file on the seat of his SUV and flipped it open again. Inside were pictures of Chance Dontay Roth. The instant the private investigator emailed him the photographs and he laid his eyes on the little boy, he knew Chance was his. His father had been right. He was the spitting image of him as a child.

Ever since he'd received the report, Darnell had been anxious to lay eyes on the child just to verify it wasn't some kind of mental trick. He had arrived at the child development center and pretended to be seeking care for an imaginary daughter just so he could see the children in the playroom and catch a glimpse up-close and personal.

In a matter of moments he had spotted Chance dashing across the playroom and the second he'd heard the raspy laughter something clutched at his heart. That familiar sound. The same sound his older brother Scott made. Nothing had prepared him for the raw emotion he'd felt when he saw his son for the first time. Darnell practically stumbled out the building and barely made it to the bushes where he puked his guts out.

How was it even possible?

He had a practice of being relatively careful, at least for the most part. He always used protection and personally disposed of his load after each performance. He'd heard of women freezing sperm and trying to insert it later with a syringe. The only time he had been a little careless had been when he'd had too much to drink to remember who she was or how he had gotten there. But how else was there to explain the mystery woman who had given birth to his child?

Darnell flipped through the report until he reached the last page and stared down at the picture of Liberty. She was butter-brown with wild dark hair and huge chocolate eyes. She was an attractive woman and he could see glimpses of his son in his mother although not as much. Chance was a Simmons thru and thru.

He sat there, staring at her photographs, memorizing every angle to memory. She didn't look like the deceptive type, but then again what did they look like. And the last time he checked women were getting more conniving by the second, which was one of the reasons why he didn't do serious relationships. The other reasons were the ones he knew were needy and looking for a husband. After a while he stopped trying to get to know women and just left things strictly about sex.

He climbed out of his Range Rover and pulled the hood of his sweatshirt over his head, blocking out the cold air as he walked across the parking lot toward the gym. From the large storefront window he could see members running on treadmills and pumping away on the elliptical machines. With determination, he headed over to the double doors and stepped inside the warmth of the building to the soft thump of Usher's recent hit circulating the room. Darnell lowered the hood from his head as he stepped up to a desk and was greeted by a receptionist. She was wearing a black uniform shirt and a nametag that read, *Paula*.

"May I help you?"

"Hello, Paula. I'm interested in information on a membership."

She nodded with excitement. "Please have a seat. Someone will be right out to give you a tour."

♥ ♥ ♥

Liberty was pecking away at her laptop when one of her fitness instructors tapped lightly at her door.

"Hey Katie, what's up?"

"Paula said there's someone waiting in the lobby interested in a tour of the facility and I can't seem to find Dana."

She nodded. "I forgot she has a doctor's appointment. Don't worry about it. I'll do it." With that Liberty finished up the last sentence of her email then hit Send. She reached for the small mirror that she kept on the end of her desk, made sure she didn't have any lettuce from her salad in her teeth, then popped a mint in her mouth as she rose.

Outside her office, she walked across the five-thousand square-foot facility. The place was in full swing. Heidi was teaching step aerobics in one of the three studios and the beat of the music was enough to make you want to jump out of your seat and participate. For an afternoon class, it was filled with members on their lunch hour for the thirty-minute segment. It had become one of the club's more popular classes.

She spotted James coming down the foyer. He was

in charge of maintenance and kept all the machines oiled and operational. "Liberty I finally got that treadmill working again."

She tossed a hand in the air. "Thank you. What would I do without you?"

He winked. "I hope you never have to find out."

Smiling, she stepped out across the workout floor. One of her personal trainers was at her left with a member on the stair climber. Liberty waved, then headed up to the reception area. One of the things she was most proud of was the people who she employed. *24/7 Fitness* was fully staffed with health and fitness experts who specialized in everything from nutrition to personal training. Every time her eyes swept the floor, she got a warm feeling inside.

It's all mine.

Who would have ever guessed she would have opened a gym? If Greg was still alive, chances were she would have still been content with just being a wife and eventually a mother, working as a personal trainer by appointments only in the studio she had set up in their basement.

When she first decided to study sports medicine, she'd planned on working with athletes, and never thought about being a fitness instructor, even though she started working as a step aerobics instructor and a personal trainer while in college. With the growing craze of aerobics and kickboxing, after Greg had died she decided to invest part of her inheritance money into a gym. And now she owned the hottest fitness center in the city.

"Hey Paula, I was told someone wants a tour?"

Nodding, she pointed to the right. "Yes, that man over there."

Liberty followed the direction of her hand and

what she saw made her startle in her breath.

He was tall, and gorgeous. No, that wasn't enough. He was sinful and yummy with skin the color of dark chestnut and powerful shoulders wide enough to belong to a professional football player. His golden-brown eyes were mesmerizing, and his lips were delicious. Then there was his short, curly hair and perfectly precision cut goatee. A sweat suit hung perfectly on his powerful build.

The gym was loud with chatter and workout equipment in use, but Liberty felt as though she and he were all alone.

What's wrong with you?

She couldn't move. Her feet felt bolted to the floor as his amber eyes roamed across her face. Her mouth became dry when his eyes drifted to her mouth, then lowered to her open cleavage, mentally stripping away her gray wrap dress and black suede pumps. Heat pulsed through her veins, and radiated into her chest. His attention came back to her face, then with deliberate ease, he rose from the chair and sauntered over her way.

Good Lord!

She swallowed. There was no ignoring the kilowatt smile that spread across his thick lips. After several breathtaking moments, she extended her hand and somehow she found the breath to say, "Hi, I'm Liberty Roth." He took her hand in his and she felt the warm heat radiate through her veins.

"Hello Liberty. I'm Darnell." His voice was smooth and dark like bars of Godiva melting over the stove. There was something familiar about his eyes. She wasn't sure what it was.

"Have we met before?" he asked as if he could read her mind.

She released his hand, and stared at him. "I was thinking the same thing. But if we have I can't remember."

Those golden eyes glinted at her as if he knew something she didn't. "Neither can I."

Liberty forced herself to shake off the effect of his intense gaze. "Darnell, let me give you a tour." She signaled for him to follow her, then turned on shaky legs. As she walked away, she could feel the heat of his gaze on her ass, making goose bumps race across her skin. For a split second, Liberty wished she had worn the pencil skirt that she had felt too lazy to iron this morning. The knit dress would just have to do. Nevertheless, she allowed her hips to sway just a little more.

"As you can see, we have a full weight room with free weights and cutting-edge circuit training and cardio equipment," she explained as they moved across the floor. "With our membership you can work out when it's best for you. Each member is given a key protected by our security system that allows you twenty-four-hour access to the front half of the building." Liberty glanced over her shoulder and was pleased to see he looked impressed.

"Do you offer kickboxing classes?"

She beamed with pride. "Yes, three mornings, weekends, and Tuesday and Thursday evening. This gym offers dozens of comprehensive Group-X and Mind/Body programming." As they passed the racquetball room, she reached for a set of double doors and swung one of them open. Darnell followed her inside the five-hundred- square-foot cycling room with thirty stationary bikes around the floor. She was telling him how popular the classes were when she swung around and swallowed hard. Darnell was staring right at her.

"Are you sure we've never met before?" Darnell said and the way he was licking his glistened lips, she nearly went into cardiac arrest. She was five-ten with three inch pumps and yet she still had to tilt her head to gaze up at him.

'"I-I don't think so." There is no way she would ever forget a man that fine.

He was standing so close she could feel his sweet warm breath against her nose. And then there was that amazing beard that was just a tad thicker than a five-o'clock shadow that her fingers were dying to reach out and touch.

"A sister..., a friend? Maybe I know your husband?" he asked, his amber eyes roaming across her face.

The mention of Greg was the splash of cold water she needed. "I doubt that. He passed away a few years ago."

"I'm sorry for your loss." The softness in his eyes told her he was sincere.

Liberty hesitated a moment. "Thank you," she whispered and then quickly changed the subject. "Let me show you where we hold kickboxing classes."

As she continued the tour, showing him the sauna room, the juice bar, and while they stopped briefly to watch, an abs class in session, Liberty watched Darnell out the corners of her eyes with fascination. He was wearing a sweat suit, the jacket was unzipped and a crisp gray t-shirt strained across his chest. She imagined underneath he was perfect with defined pecs and a six-pack of abs. She had the sudden urge to reach out and touch him, which was ridiculous. When it came to potential members she was always all about business. Never flirted or felt an inkling of attraction, but there was something about this man that had her nipples beading and her hands sweating. *Maybe offering him a membership wasn't such a good idea,* she wondered.

♥ ♥ ♥

By the time Liberty escorted him toward the back to her office, Darnell had to admit he was definitely impressed with the gym. Especially when the real reason for coming wasn't to join the gym, instead it was to see the owner up-close and personal and see if he remembered her. And he did not.

As he followed the sway of her wide hips, he released a long breath. Liberty was breathtakingly beautiful with a narrow waist and an ass that he would have trailed to the west coast.

For the life of him he couldn't understand how he couldn't remember those long shapely legs and a walk that was potent enough to stop a man's heart. Sure, he'd dated and bedded dozens of women but he never, and he meant never forgot a pretty face. Now names were a different story all together, however with a name like Liberty it wasn't likely.

"Come on in and have a seat." She pushed open a door and he followed her inside the small room and he watched her round an oak desk and lower onto the seat. Her sweet perfume surrounded him and he felt intoxicated in a way he hadn't felt since before he'd stopped drinking.

With his eyes on her, he dropped onto the chair across from her desk.

"So, now that you've seen our facilities do you think it will work for your lifestyle?" she said on a breath.

His eyes moved back and forth across her face, memorizing every detail from the length of her thick lashes to the fullness of her red painted lips. "That depends."

"Depends on what?" she asked, angling her head to one side.

"My schedule," he replied then slid down comfortably on the seat. "I need something as flexible as possible and I think twenty-four hour access to the front of the facility is exactly what I'm looking for. Now I'll just have to learn how to work it in my business schedule."

Smiling, she nodded and said, "What kind of work do you do?"

"I'm an attorney."

Her brown eyes flashed with interest. *As if she didn't already know.* "Really? What kind?"

Darnell decided to play along. "My cousins and I specialize in family law."

Her lips curled flirtatiously. "I'm impressed."

"Thank you," he said and stretched trying to shake off the effect of her smile. Why was she continuing to pretend she didn't know him? he pondered. "Do you have gift certificates? I would like to give them to my family for Christmas."

She nodded. "Sure. We have gift cards that can be used to participate in any twenty of our Group-X classes with no membership required. Although, I'm hoping if they attend they will eventually join." Liberty fluttered her thick lashes and caused his groin to grow tight.

"I'll take three." He was sure his sister would use the gift as long as he bought one for his sister-in-law Zanaa and his father's wife Jennifer as well. The three women were always doing something together.

Liberty opened a manila folder on her desk and took out a form. "While I get your gift certificates ready, I need you to fill out this membership application. Then I'll need either a voided check or a credit card for automatic bank drafts."

Nodding, Darnell took the small five-by-seven card from her, along with a personalized pen and started filling in the blanks. He glanced over to the shelf behind her and spotted the photo on the shelf behind her that made his heart pound. "Who's lil' man is that?" he asked and saw the way her face lit up with pride.

"That's my son, Chance." Liberty reached for the picture and gazed down at it lovingly before turning it around so he could get a closer look. Why was she taunting him like this when she knew good and damn well that was his son?

My son.

Their son.

Anger started brimming at the surface, but he maintained his focus on the index card. "Raising a boy is hard work…, especially without a father," he said while watching her out the corner of his eye.

He noticed the brief moment of sadness and almost felt bad for bringing up something painful, but now was not the time to feel sorry for her. She was playing games and he was determined to find out why.

She shook her head slowly, sending her wild curls bouncing as she blinked back into the present. "Yeah, Chance can be a real handful," she commented with a weary smile. "But he's *all* boy and I just love it," she added and giggled.

He lifted an eyebrow. "What do you mean?"

She propped an elbow on the table and rested her chin in her palm. "Baseball, action figures, running, playing. That boy has so much heart."

Looking up from the form, Darnell grinned.

"Sound like you got the makings of an all-American."

There was that cute smirk again. He felt another stir at his groin and shifted on the seat. "I sure hope so. I can't wait until he's old enough for me to sign up at the recreation center."

"I remember my days at the rec center. You name it, me and my brother were doing it." He signed his name to the form, then slid it across her desk along with his credit card.

"Thank you and here you go." She handed him three small cream envelopes with red bows. "Very nice Christmas presents. Although..."

One thick brow lifted. "Although what?"

She flashed him a look and the part of his anatomy he couldn't control suffered another tight, near painful pull. "You said they're for the women in your life? Well, a woman could think you're trying to tell her something."

He paused a moment until the light went on in his head. "Damn, I didn't think about that." Sheyna would be the first to say he was trying to call her fat. "Oh well, my sister will have to get over it," he said with a chuckle.

She giggled along with him and he felt a shiver pulse through his vein at the sound. "Oh darn! I'm out of welcome packages. I'll be right back."

He nodded as she reached for his credit card, rose and walked out the room. Once again, he was hit by another surge of sexual hunger he'd experienced at first sight at the welcome desk.

After she left, he reached over and picked up the picture of his son and gazed down at his familiar face. How long was she going to pretend she didn't know him or that this wasn't his son?

And why the hell was he attracted to the enemy?

he scolded. Yet there was no denying that he liked what he saw. The pictures the private investigator had given him, hadn't done her justice. They were nothing like the Liberty Roth up-close and personal.

Dammit!

She was beautiful and perfect, with butter-brown delicate skin, dark-brown wild spiral hair, and large, dark sultry eyes. The sweater dress clung to slender arms and hugged large round breasts, while her hips and ass flared enough to confirm she was all woman. A combination as potent as chilled tequila with a kick of heat spread like wildfire through his blood.

Just thinking about what he could do with a body like that had his groin humming and ready to give in to his reckless desire. It took everything he had to hold onto that thread of anger and then he shook his head and asked that question again. What kind of game was she playing? Or maybe she wasn't playing and she had no intention of ever telling him Chance was his son. Well, too bad. Maybe there were some men out there who didn't have a problem stepping away from their responsibility, but not Darnell Simmons. Nothing or no one would ever stop him from being a part of his son's life.

Liberty stepped back into her office, smiling innocently over at him as she returned to her seat. "All right I think you're all set. And here is your membership t-shirt." She held out a navy blue t-shirt with the gym's logo. He forced a smile and took it from her proffered hand.

"This is your swipe card. When you have time drop by the front desk so we can take your picture. This will also be used for twenty-four hour access through the side door that I showed you."

He nodded and drew in a long breath.

"And that's it. Welcome to *24/7 Fitness!*" she said, smiling. "Do you have any questions for me?"

He did, but Darnell decided now was not the time. "No, I think you've answered everything."

"If you do I'm here almost every day. If not, my staff can get in touch with me," she explained and then there was a brief pause and he felt that electric pull again.

Liberty smiled. "Well, if that's all, then let me walk you out."

He followed the sway of her hips out the door.

Darnell had all the information he needed, and he was already anticipating them meeting again very soon under different circumstances.

♥ ♥ ♥

Liberty went back to her office. The scent of Darnell still lingered in the room. Goodness that man was gorgeous.

She lowered back into her seat and took a moment to relive the moments she had spent with him. As a rule she never mixed business and pleasure with her members, at least not intentionally, and there was something about that gorgeous man that had her thinking about breaking the rules.

With a giggle she pushed aside the crazy thought. A man that fine had a string of women already on speed dial and she definitely wasn't interested in being a part of a harem. After all he did buy gift cards for the *women* in his life.

She heard a soft knock at the door and looked up to see Cash standing in the doorway. "Hey you."

She sashayed in wearing a pair of pink scrubs covered with brown bears on them. "Did you see that delicious-looking man who just walked out the building?" she said pointing out toward the lobby.

Liberty didn't even have to ask her to describe him to know she was talking about Darnell. "He's a new member."

"Holy smoke!" she said on a breath and flopped down onto the chair across from her desk. "Please tell me he's single."

She shrugged. "I'm not sure. He signed up for a single gym membership but he bought gift cards for three women."

Cash leaned closer. "Well at least he knows how to treat the ladies."

Yes, she had a feeling he knew his way with women. In fact Liberty was certain sex with him would be unforgettable. Something about Darnell Simmons shouted confident in everything he did.

"He asked about the kickboxing classes."

Her dark eyes sparkled. "Then I guess I will definitely see him again. Did you tell him you're the instructor?"

Liberty shook her head.

"I'll make sure to wear something extra tight the next time I attend your class." Suddenly her eyes narrowed. "Unless you were thinking about…"

"No way. You can have him." The last thing she needed was a pretty boy. Men like him were good to look at, but nothing more. But that didn't stop her from anticipating seeing Darnell again.

Chapter Four

"Do you think I have a chance?"

"I know you do," Darnell told him confidently.

There was no disguising the worry still lingering in his client's gaze. "You sound so sure."

He sent him a signature smile and leaned closer. "If I wasn't, would you want me representing you?"

Mr. Larsen's shoulders relaxed with laughter. "I guess you do have a point."

Darnell chuckled along with his new client and once he sobered, discussed strategy until Mr. Larsen seemed at ease. A few minutes later, Darnell swirled around on his office chair as he watched him leave his spacious corner office at Simmons, Simmons & Simmons, L.L.P.

An hour ago, Mr. Larsen had been practically in tears as he explained how he had been battling his ex-wife to see his son for over ten years. All the deadbeat fathers out there and here was a man who wanted nothing more than to be with his son. When he'd asked about having joint custody and reducing the amount of child support that was being garnished from his check, his ex-wife got livid and made it clear it would never happen. After spending time with his son on Sunday and dropping him back off at home, the cops showed up to Mr. Larsen's house and arrested him. According to the ex-wife, he had beaten their son, even though there was no visible evidence. Now his new client was not only facing criminal charges but his ex was demanding sole custody of their thirteen-year-old son, and until social services did a full investigations he wasn't allowed anywhere near the boy.

Not if I could help it.

A guardian ad litem had been appointed to represent the best interest of the kid. Darnell knew Christopher Weber quite well and knew the attorney's main priority would be Mr. Larsen's son. The ex-wife was being represented by Janna Forrest, a bulldog that Darnell had come up against several times in court. Her strategy was drawing sympathy for her client.

Not this time.

He would do everything in his power to make sure all the charges were dropped so his client could resume being a part of his son's life.

Darnell pushed up from the chair and paced the length of his elegantly furnished office with his fist balled at his side in anger.

It was cases like these that were the reason why he didn't want any part of marriage or children. One moment the couple's inseparable and in the next they were clawing at each other's throats.

As he gazed out the window, he thought about his own personal life. A few months ago, Tori who he'd been dating for almost a year had suddenly called it quits, accusing him of caring about his career more than he did her. Sure he worked a lot of long hours, but he always found time for her. She knew Darnell wasn't interested in anything serious, but he thought they had an understanding that worked well for both of them. He believed it was about the quality not the quantity and thought as an owner of a floral shop she understood, but apparently she hadn't. During dinner one evening she told him she wanted more from their relationship, and when he didn't respond the way she had expected, Tori got up from the table and he'd never seen her again.

Anyone who knew him knew he didn't do ultimatums and a commitment was the last thing he wanted. In the end, Darnell chucked it off as a loss and kept on course. He was on the fast track to becoming one of the best family law attorneys in the state and he knew that required making sacrifices, and being a little bit selfish from time to time.

But now that he had a son things had to be different.

The last two days he had been tortured with thoughts of not only Chance, but also his mother. The sway of her hips, the shape of her succulent looking breasts and that saucy grin. At times, his thoughts were so erotic it left his penis thick and hard. He had to give himself a mental scolding because those were not the feelings he wanted to have for a woman who had denied him an opportunity to know his son and be a part of his life. Nothing about Liberty seemed selfish or vindictive and yet what else could there be? Unknowingly he must have broken her heart or maybe he told her he wanted nothing to do with a wife or a family. And that was true before he found out about Chance. But once Liberty discovered she was pregnant and made the decision to keep the baby, she should have told him because even though he wouldn't have been pleased, he would have supported her decision. He believed a woman had the right to make their own decisions about their body. However, he had a right to know.

Dammit, he muttered under his breath. Why couldn't he remember her? He didn't know why it bothered him as it did. Especially knowing at some point they had been lovers with his cock buried deep between her lush thighs. Feeling heat flowing to his groin, he gave himself a mental shake and pushed aside the thought. Sex was the last thing he needed to think about. Instead he needed to focus on figuring out what kind of game she was playing. He had been at the gym, and not once did she give any indication she knew him. She was good. He'd give her that. But what she didn't know was he had been up against women like her before, conniving, vindictive, like his new client's ex-wife. And one thing she didn't know about Darnell Simmons was that he loved a challenge.

He stared out the window, blood boiling hot through his veins. It was the same blood that ran through Chance. A child that had been living barely a fifteen-minute drive from his home for the last three years. He cussed under his breath. If it hadn't been for his father, he never would have known he had a son living right in Sheraton Beach. As a result, he'd missed out on so much.

But not anymore.

His golden eyes glittered with determination. Nothing was going to stop him from being in his life. Nothing. But after meeting Liberty it was crystal clear, it wasn't going to be easy. The woman was passionate about her business, intelligent, and as a saleswoman, she didn't easily back down. It was apparent she was tough and he was going to have a battle on his hands.

And he was ready.

♥ ♥ ♥

"Good night Boo-Boo."

"Night, Mommy."

Liberty kissed Chance's chubby cheek, then watched as he turned over onto his side and closed his eyes. Grinning, she pulled the covers up and tucked him in. After a long day, he was going to be sound asleep within minutes.

She turned out the lamp, then walked over to the door and didn't make any effort to leave. Instead she stood in the doorway and gazed over at her pride and joy.

Greg would have been so proud.

He used to talk all the time about having a son. Someone he could teach to play baseball, and to take fishing, and a son who could carry on the family name. Before she had discovered she was pregnant with Chance, she'd had two miscarriages and each time Greg was just as devastated as she had been, maybe even more, which was why she had chosen to wait to tell him she was pregnant with Chance. Now she wished she hadn't waited and had told him, just to have seen the look on his face. It would at least have been a story she could have shared with Chance, again and again. Especially since he'd been asking about his daddy.

Liberty blinked back tears and pulled his bedroom door slightly closed, then padded quietly down the stairs of the small Cape Cod house. She then strolled through the living room into the galley-style kitchen.

While making a cup of peppermint tea she leaned her hips against the counter and glanced around the room. Peeling wallpaper was a constant reminder of all the DIY projects she planned on tackling when she'd first bought the three-bedroom fixer-upper, but time was never something she had much of with the gym and a little boy running around. Plans were already topping the list of her New Year's Resolution.

Just as the microwave timer went off, the doorbell rang disturbing her thoughts.

Liberty pushed away from the counter and hurried before the bell disturbed Chance. Not bothering to look in the peephole, she yanked open the front door and then gasped in surprise when she saw who was standing there.

Darnell.

She wasn't sure why she remembered his name but she did. Probably because of how fine he was, she thought as her heart thundered in her chest. Was he really standing at her doorstep or had her mind conjured him up since she'd thought of him often the last few days?

"Darnell… can I help you?"

"Actually Liberty, you can." Without waiting for an invitation Darnell stepped inside the house, causing her to gasp. *What the…*

She called after him. "I didn't invite you—"

"No, but we need to talk." Without waiting for a response he strolled into the living room.

Why was Darnell in her house? Liberty hurried to shut the door and stormed into the living room to find him standing near her shelf holding a picture of Chance talking with his coach at summer camp. Her maternal instincts kicked in.

"What do you want?" she asked tapping her foot impatiently and suddenly was having second thoughts about letting him in her house with Chance sleeping upstairs.

She moved closer to the umbrella on the side of the couch, prepared to grab it and swing if needed. "I asked a question. What do you want?"

"When was this picture taken?" he asked, looking at her while pointing at the photograph. With purposeful strides, she stormed over and practically snatched the photo from him.

"That's none of your business!"

He gave a rude snort. "No. I'm afraid that it is my business and would appreciate it if you would quit playing games and answer the question."

"Excuse me? You're the one who came barging into my house!" she spat.

"Because I want answers."

Oh God, he smelled incredible. Seeing him again, threw her for a loop, but now that she had recovered from the shock, she was anxious to send him out her front door again. "What answers?" Liberty asked, while stepping backwards. "Does this have something to do with your membership? If there's a problem we can talk about it at my office tomorrow."

"This has nothing to do with my membership," he snarled, then gave her a long hard look that caused her to take another step back. "Why are you acting like we haven't met before and you don't know who I am?"

Liberty shook off the effect of his cologne as her chin came up in a challenge. "Because I don't."

He stared at her eyes probing like he thought she was lying. "I'm serious. I have no idea who you are."

He chuckled and returned the photo to the shelf then had the nerve to shrug out of his dark brown leather jacket as if he'd been invited to stay. "See... this is why I don't do relationships. Y'all women play too many games."

Her mouth dropped. "*Y'all women?*"

Nodding, he draped his jacked across the arm of her couch. "Yeah, you heard me.

"Well this woman doesn't' know what gave you the idea you could just come up in here making demands. I said I never met you before, so you either get outta my house or I'm calling the police." With that Liberty pivoted on her toes and stormed to the door, only to her dismay he didn't follow.

"I'm not going anywhere until we talk," Darnell called after her, and although his words were soft there was a lethal calmness that caused her body to shiver.

Liberty swore under her breath then walked back into the room to find Darnell seated on her blue loveseat. For some odd reason, she wasn't afraid of him, nor had he given her any reason to think he'd do her bodily harm, nevertheless, the sooner he was gone the better.

She stood in the doorway, her fists knotted at her sides and shoulders back. "I told you I have no idea who you are so I don't know what it is you want!"

There was that confident look again.

"Liberty," he began, then shook his head. "We both know I'm here about Chance."

Her breath stalled. "Chance? Why are you here about my son?"

Darnell dragged a hand across his head. "Listen, Liberty. I know I can be an ass, and some people call me selfish, but believe me when I tell you, I'm sorry for seducing you and not calling you back."

"Seducing me? When did you *seduce* me?"

"Okay, I guess I phrased that wrong. 'Had sex with you.'" He tossed quotation marks in the air. "Whatever you want to call it. Just so you'll know, it's not you… it's me."

Liberty shook her head, growing more confused by the second and moved over and took a seat. "What are you talking about?"

"I'm talking about the way I treated you," he began. "I'll admit a few years ago I did have a bit of a drinking problem and half the time I couldn't remember who or what I did the night before," he spoke slow and precise and she caught herself watching his lips. "But I'm not that man anymore. Well... at least the excessive drinking part. What I'm trying to say is I'm sorry for misleading you and making you feel so used you couldn't even come and tell me you were carrying my son."

His words stifled the power for her to speak. *Son?*

She sucked in a shocked voice and said, "What makes you think Chance is your son?"

Darnell cracked out a laugh. "Come on. There are too many similarities. I saw the way he walks and that silly way he smiles when he wants something and then —"

"Wait a minute, you've been watching him?"

He was quiet, thinking carefully about his answer. "I hired someone to track you both down."

"What?" She sprung from the chair. "Why?"

"Liberty, playing games isn't my style," he said accusingly. "I take family way too serious for that." Darnell paused and rested his hands on his knees as he leaned forward. "Just tell me where we met and get on with this. He's my kid. You and I both know it."

"My son has a father."

"Who? Your deceased husband?" he snarled.

She paused, unable to respond. Darnell was way too arrogant and hurtful for his own good.

"I'm sorry. That didn't come out right," he said and his eyes had softened a bit.

She nodded, but didn't dare speak.

He drew a deep breath and closed his eyes briefly. "Listen Liberty... I don't know why you won't tell me where we met. And that's cool. You don't have to. All I care about is my son."

"Son? Don't be ridiculous. Chance isn't your son. Before you walked into my gym I never saw you before in my life."

Now Darnell looked frustrated before he shook his head in disbelief. "I think you're lying."

Another jolt of anger pulsed through her. She had way too much integrity to just sit there and let him call her a liar. Instantly, she sprung from the chair. "I *think* it's time you leave and if you don't I'm calling the police."

He rose from the loveseat, walked over and his arm curled around hers, twirling her in a circle, and the next thing Liberty knew, she'd collided with Darnell's hot, hard body.

"Tell me the truth, otherwise, I will see you in court. Nothing or no one is going to keep me away from my son."

Liberty glared up into those familiar amber eyes. Darnell tilted his head and what she saw caused her jaw to drop.

"Is... is that a birthmark?"

"Yes ... in the shape of Louisiana. Just like your son's."

It took a moment for what he was saying to register and then it hit her. "Nooo!" Her eyes widened. She backed away as if she had suddenly been burned.

Silence filled the room while she moved over to the window and stared out at the snow that was starting to fall. Her eyelids lowered as she tried to take a moment to process it all.

"Why didn't you tell me about him?" he asked, breaking the silence.

Liberty looked over her shoulder at him. "Because I didn't know who his father was."

His eyes were narrowed suspiciously. "What do you mean you didn't know who I was?"

She folded her arms in front of her and started pacing the room. "First off, I don't even know how any of this is even possible."

Liberty could see the frustration on his face and now she understood why. She walked around the coffee table and lowered on the ottoman. "I got pregnant through artificial insemination. So unless you donated to a sperm bank in Illinois, Chance is not your son," she challenged.

Darnell stilled, every ounce of blood in his face draining away, and when he walked over to the couch and took a seat, he confirmed her worst nightmare.

Darnell Simmons was Chance's father.

Panic seized her. "W-what were you doing in Illinois?"

"I attended Northwestern." He sat back on the couch, his golden eyes reflecting his despair. "Are you from Illinois? I'm mean... what ... hell I don't know what I mean."

She flinched but remained proud. "My husband was doing a PhD program at Northwestern."

"And why were you at a sperm bank?" His tone demanded answers.

She tilted her chin. "That's a private matter."

There was a tense silence before Darnell pressed on. "How did you end up here in Sheraton Beach?"

"My best friend lives here."

A muscle at his jaw flexed with fury. "If you hadn't moved here I never would have known about my son."

"He's *not* your son! He's mine. His last name is Roth just like my husband."

His eyes were fixed on hers as he laughed. "We both know Chance isn't his son."

The pain from her past came rushing back. "According to his birth certificate he is, and I'd like to keep it that way."

"The hell we are!" he shouted and jerked up from

the couch. "That's my son and I want a chance to be a part of his life."

She shook her head. "You have no rights to my son and the last thing I want to do is confuse him." Liberty stood as well. "Now I really would appreciate it if you would leave my house."

His eyes veiled any hint of his carefully concealed emotion.

"I'm not leaving until we discuss my parental rights."

Her stomach clenched. "Rights? You're a sperm donor, so you have no rights."

She stared him down for a long moment before he gave a cross between a snort and a laugh. "You forget I'm a lawyer and I won't hesitate to drag you to court if I have to."

Heat suffused her face. "*What?* Why would you do that?" Her voice cracked a little.

"Because I want to be a part of my son's life. Can't you understand that?"

She was breathing hard as she spat, "All I know is that you show up at my house making demands and if you don't leave now I really am calling the police... I mean it."

"Mommy."

She stilled, cringing as she heard Chance calling her name. Why? Why now? How was it possible he had climbed of bed in search of her at this exact moment?

They both turned and there he was standing at the bottom of the stairs, rubbing his eyes.

"Boo-Boo what are you doing up?" she said as she walked over and stroked his curly hair.

"I'm hungry," Chance replied, rubbed his eyes, then tilted his head and stared up at Darnell. "Hi," he said shyly.

Darnell gazed down at him and then let out a long breath. "Hello." Liberty noticed how soft his voice had gotten. "How are you lil' man?"

"Hungry."

Darnell rumbled with laughter, then dropped down on one knee in front of him and held out his hand. "I'm Dee ... a friend of your mother." She watched as his large hand swallowed up her son's.

"My name's Chance."

"Hello Chance. It's nice to finally meet you."

Panic rose in her chest. "Chance, this is *Mr. Dee.*" She turned to him eyes blazing, hands shaking. "And he's just leaving," she added through gritted teeth.

Liberty could tell Darnell was about to say something more when she lifted a hand and cut him off. "Please." Her voice was shaking.

Darnell let out his breath in an impatient hiss then rose to his feet. And when his eyes took her in, her traitorous body betrayed her. Heat flooded her. Her nipples became tight under his penetrating stare yet at the same time fear weakened her knees. How was it possible for her to lust after someone who was threatening to destroy her life?

With a reluctant nod, Darnell retrieved his leather jacket and headed to the door. She took Chance's hand into hers and stepped out of his way as he walked across the foyer to the front door. With a hand on the doorknob, Darnell turned his head and said with stiff authority, "I meant what I said, Liberty. I have every intention of being a part of my son's life."

Chapter Five

The following morning, Darnell marched down the plush hall of the law firm to his cousin's office at the far left, and knocked once, then stuck his head in. Once he made sure Dax Simmons wasn't on the phone with a client, he barged inside. "I need to talk to you."

Dax leaned back on the chair his dark eyes fixed. "Sure. What's up?'

A few years younger, Dax was the older of his two partners, who were twin brothers and his first cousins. The paper-bag brown colored man was the most level-headed of all of them which was why Darnell decided to talk to him instead of Patrick who hadn't made it into the office yet.

In the past, he would have gone to his big brother for advice but ever since Scott and Zanaa had hooked up, everything that came out of that dude's mouth was all about love and family. Two things he wanted nothing to do with.

"Before you get started, how'd things go in court this morning?"

"A slam dunk," Darnell murmured. His client had been more interested in winning custody of his dog rather than his three children. His wife already had the dog in the car, ready to deliver to him.

He straddled the chair in front of him, then tossed a manila folder onto the desk. "Look at that."

Dax stared at him before lowering his gaze to the folder. "What is it?"

"Look and see," Darnell said impatiently.

He hesitated a moment then he finally reached down for the file and thumbed through it.

His eyes lit up with recognition. "This is the chick Uncle Shaun was talking about. Liberty Roth?"

"Yep." He nodded and pointed to the folder, encouraging him to keep looking. "That's her."

While Dax leafed through all the information, he sprung from the chair and gazed out onto the busy Dover shopping district. He loved the area but compared to Sheraton Beach it was a poor substitute. Growing up he never guessed he would miss living near the ocean, but in the last year since he'd stopped drinking, his life slowed down. He'd realized just how lucky he was to live in the small ocean view town, which was well worth the thirty-minute daily commute to work. In fact, last year, he had sold his condominium, and purchased a three-thousand square foot home in Sheraton Beach when the market was just too good to resist.

While waiting, Darnell occasionally glanced over at Dax looking for some idea of what he was thinking, and when he got nothing, he scowled. His cousin always did take a calm approach, making it hard at times to read him.

When he had first started his law firm, Darnell knew he wanted the twins to come and work with him. They graduated the top of their class at Cornell University and before they had even passed the bar, he was recruiting them hard to partner with him. And not a single day had he regretted his decision. They were all bachelors and yet they knew how to keep work and play separate. The twins were just as passionate about family law as he was and together Simmons, Simmons & Simmons was a force to be reckoned with.

Dax finally lowered the file and Darnell tapped his hand impatiently against his thigh as he waited for his response.

His brow bunched with confusion as he said, "I don't see what the problem is. This woman was artificially inseminated, which means Uncle Shaun was wrong and you just dodged having a baby mama." Dax stuck out his hand for a fist bump that his cousin ignored.

"*Wrong.*" Darnell shook his head "Pops was right. That's my son."

Frowning, Dax lowered his hand and looked down at the document on top. "I must be missing something because I don't see how he could be your son, unless you were making deposits at a sperm bank in Chicago, Illinois." He chuckled and then suddenly his eyes widened. "Chicago? While you were in college ..." he allowed the rest of his sentence to trail off as he saw the answer in his cousin's eye, and winced. "Oh snap!"

"I needed to pay for lab fees my junior year. Dad's check was tight and it was the only way I could pay for it." He dragged a frustrated hand across his hair. "I only did it that one time."

"And I bet you never imagined it to come back and bite you in the ass." Disbelief was written all over his cousin's brown face as he shook his head.

Darnell's jaw tightened while he leaned back in his chair, eyes dark and watchful.

After a long moment, Dax leaned forward, elbows on the desk. "How did you get this information, a private investigator?"

He nodded.

"What are you planning to do?"

"I'm going to sue for visitation rights."

"But you don't have any rights," Dax pointed out quietly, his tone reasonable. "That's why it's called "sperm donating."

"So you don't think a judge in this city will listen to my case?" he asked, eyes narrowed.

Dax blew out a long breath. "I'm not saying they won't listen, but sperm donating is a contentious subject. Dee, you're talking about a long drawn-out case, especially if Liberty is a good mother."

He had no doubt in his mind she was a good mother. The house had been clean and there were toys scattered neatly around the room. "He's my son," he insisted.

Dax held his gaze. "No, he's her son. You have no rights. Your donation was done through an agency. We're not talking about a one-night stand. As a sperm donor you automatically lost all claims to the child, and being that his mother was married, the husband automatically became the legal father."

"I don't agree." He impatiently shifted on the seat.

"You always were stubborn," Dax muttered and cupped his bearded chin with long masculine fingers — a habit of his whenever he was thinking. "Have you tried talking to her?"

"Yes and she doesn't want me to see him."

He looked him straight in the eyes. "Did she say why?"

His face flamed at the reminder. "Probably because I did come off like an ass." At his cousin's surprised look, Darnell leaned back on the chair and told him how he first faked a gym membership then appeared at her doorstep calling her a liar. At the end Darnell shook his head while Dax leaned forward, elbows on the desk and hands steepled.

"Dee look, you can take her to court but I guarantee it's going to be long and emotionally draining, and in the end, the outcome far worse. You don't want that."

"I plan to be in his life," he countered, not at all conceding.

"I understand that. But you've been a lawyer long enough to know the battle for custody can be among the ugliest and most heart-breaking legal battles you will ever face. You'll not only be hurting his mother, but the boy as well."

Darnell scrubbed a hand over his face, then exhaled a deep breath. He definitely didn't want that because if he did and failed, Liberty wasn't going to ever allow him anywhere near the boy.

He rose and started pacing again as he thought about how she had stood up to him. He had accused her of being a liar who intentionally kept his son from him. And when he attacked, she struck back like a lioness with a cub. Guilt pricked his conscious as Darnell thought about how wrong he had been. He had always been a good judge of character, but this time he had been way off base. Liberty was no liar. She'd had no idea he was Chance's father and her surprise at the discovery was truly genuine. Just thinking about the way he had treated her, made him feel like an ass for sure. If his father ever caught wind of what he had done, he would truly be disappointed.

Darnell lowered his eyelids and the fire in her gaze became visual. Liberty Roth was no pushover, especially when it was something she was passionate about. And passion was the word that came to mind every time he thought about those lush curves and the slight fullness of her lower lip.

Liberty was gorgeous. And as much as he didn't want to think of his son's mother that way, he couldn't deny the way she made him feel every time he was near her. Even the heated debate had his body totally hard and his cock jutting against the zipper of his slacks by the time he'd strolled out the door.

"I've got a plan if you're willing to listen," he heard his cousin say.

Darnell stopped and turned around, heaving a heavy sigh. "Sure. I'll do whatever it takes to be with my son."

"Then pull up a chair and let the master work his magic," Dax replied with a wicked smirk.

♥ ♥ ♥

"*He's your sperm donor?*" Cash gasped and immediately covered her mouth with her hand.

Liberty sprung from the chair and hurried to shut the door to her office. "Lower your voice," she murmured.

"Oops sorry," she said apologetically as she wiggled out of the floor-length wool coat, showing her pink nursery scrubs underneath. Cash waited until Liberty returned to her seat before saying. "Are you sure?"

She groaned inward and it pained her to nod her head. "Yes, I'm afraid so."

Cash shook her head with increased confusion. "But you were inseminated in Chicago."

She nodded. "With sperm Darnell donated while in college."

"What's the likelihood of something like that happening?" she asked, her big brown eyes bulging wide as she studied her.

"Virtually impossible," Liberty replied.

She and her husband had moved to Chicago after Greg was accepted in the Kellogg Doctoral Program at

Northwestern University. A smile curled her lips as she remembered how happy they had been. It seemed the only thing missing was a baby.

They'd tried to conceive for almost two years before they went to see a fertility doctor and discovered Greg's sperm count was too low to ever father a child. Her husband knew how badly she had wanted a baby and had eventually agreed to artificial insemination with donor sperm. Liberty had already miscarried twice before she discovered she was pregnant with Chance, and after two heartaches she decided to wait until she had made it past the first trimester before she allowed herself to get excited. After Greg's death, Cash encouraged Liberty she needed a change and suggested she move to Delaware so she could have a support system.

Liberty wagged her head with disbelief. She had no idea her decision had brought her to the same town as her sperm donor.

"How did he find out?" Cash asked, as she pulled a hamburger out of a brown bag and brought it to her lips.

"I don't know how he found out. All I know for sure, is Chance looks just like him." She paused long enough to shake her weary head again. "I knew there was something about him that was familiar. I had no idea it was because he and my son were related. He even has the same Louisiana-shaped birthmark behind his left ear."

Cash stilled and for once was speechless.

Liberty sighed. "I know. It's crazy, right?"

"Beyond crazy." She managed and resumed chewing. "So now that he knows, what is he planning to do?"

Remembering the cruel way in which he'd

delivered his threats the night before, she replied, "He wants parental rights, which I was quick to point out he didn't have any." Her tone was harsh.

"Maybe so ... but..."

Her gaze narrowed. "But what? I don't know this dude and he's going to just pop up on my door and accuse me of being some hoochie that slept with him and had his baby without his knowledge."

Cash shot her an incredulous look. "He said that?"

She looked at her friend for a moment and let out a long suffering sigh. "He implied that I was playing games. When I told him Chance was conceived artificially you should have seen the color wash away from his face."

Cash gave a look of wry amusement. "*That dark chocolate morsel*? I would have loved to have seen that."

Liberty's insides tingled with pleasure at the thought of all that chocolate testosterone standing on her doorstep. Waving her hand in the air, she tried to shake off the effect. "Anyway, I told him he didn't have a legal leg to stand on and then put him out my house."

"This is better than watching *The Young and the Restless* at lunch time!" Cash was looking at her closely. "And then what did he say?"

Liberty sighed as she tugged a strand of hair behind her ear. "He told me he's an attorney and he'd be back."

"Wow! An attorney." Cash gave her first weary look since she'd arrive. "Does he really have no legal rights?"

She felt sick as she shrugged. "I don't know. I really don't know." And that's what she feared the most. "What man would tear a child from his mother's love?"

Ever since he came knocking at her door Liberty couldn't stop worrying. No matter how often she told herself he had no rights, she couldn't get her mind to settle down. All she'd been doing was wondering what Darnell might be up to. She even got up this morning trying to figure his plan out, and it was driving her crazy. For all she knew he had already hired a lawyer. Hell, he hired a private investigator so she didn't put anything past him. But after he retained a lawyer then what? Even if he didn't have any legal right, Darnell seemed like the type of man who would make her life a living hell until he got what he wanted. *Her son.* There was no way in hell she was allowing him to take her son from her.

Cash must have sensed her frustrations because she reached over and patted her hand. "Girl, no worries. You are a damn good mother and I can get enough people to fill up this gym who will vouch for you."

"Thanks." She wasn't sure what she would do without her and hoped she never had to find out.

A quick glance down at her watch indicated she had a class in thirty minutes. When Cash called to say she would be by for lunch, Liberty decided to go in the ladies locker room and change into leggings and her black 24/7 *Fitness* t-shirt to save time.

There was a long moment of silence and she looked over to see Cash staring at her funny. "What?"

"You know… It's really not a bad idea."

Liberty drew back and glared over at her suspiciously. "What's not a bad idea?"

"Allowing Darnell to be a father to his child."

"Are you serious!" She couldn't believe what Cash was saying.

Cash nodded and reached for her drink as she said, "I'm serious. He needs a father. Why not the man who's actually his father?"

"He's not a father! He's just a sperm donor," she hissed defensively. If anyone should understand, it should have been her best friend.

"Yeah, but he's a donor who wants to be a father to his sperm, and a *fine* piece of sperm if I say so myself." Cash gave her a weird look and then exploded with laughter. "Okay, that probably sounded crazy. But I'm serious. I mean just think about it. Chance needs a father and what better person than the blood that runs through his veins?"

She blinked rapidly and didn't bother to respond.

"I think you should at least give the man a chance," Cash egged on.

Liberty bit her lip and twisted her hands together anxiously. "I don't know anything about him."

"Okay, then let's google him and see what we find out." She plopped down her cup then reached for a smart phone from her purse. "What's his last name?"

"Hold on." Liberty thumbed through her middle desk drawer until she found his enrollment application. "Simmons. His name is Darnell Simmons."

"Hmmm, let's see."

Liberty waited while Cash typed rapidly into the phone, and was practically gnawing the inside of her cheek. She didn't know why she was nervous at what she might find out. Probably because whatever she discovered might someday affect her son. "I don't think I want to know."

After a few moments, Cash's eyes brightened. Oh, you're gonna want to know this! "He practices family law."

"What!" she gasped, outraged.

"Uh-huh. Up in Dover at Simmons Simmons & Simmons, L.L.P. It must be a family law firm."

Family. Something she couldn't give her son. Did she really want to deprive Chance of that?

"He does pro-bono work all the time. Volunteers with Habitat for Humanity ... Oh my goodness! He's the brother of Scott Simmons."

Her brow rose. The name didn't sound familiar. "Scott Simmons?"

"The videogame creator. I remember reading he sold a design last year for over five million." Cash was clearly impressed. The thought had her shaking in her UGG boots. It just meant that money wouldn't be an object if he had his brother's support.

"He attended Northwestern."

The same place where Greg had accepted a PhD program, studying economics. The same city where Chance had been fertilized on a petri dish. "Yes, he told me that."

"And check this out! Guess who his sister is married to?" she shrieked.

Liberty shrugged. She didn't have a clue, and was almost afraid to ask. "Who?"

"Jace Beaumont."

Her heart sank. The Beaumonts. The most influential family in the area. Jace was the oldest, and also the director of human resources for the Beaumont Corporation. Five-star resorts at its best. The Sheraton Beach location was responsible for providing hundreds of jobs to local residents.

"I'm sorry but I don't see anything about this man that would make you raise a red flag. Chance is one lucky kid." There was no mistake Cash was impressed.

Traitor.

And yet she had to admit, other than her undying love and devotion, Darnell Simmons had so much more to offer her son than she ever could, and he came from a large extended family. How could she continue to say no to that?

She caught Cash looking at her, eyes narrowed with concern. "What's running through your mind?"

Liberty stared at her for several moments, then shifted on the seat and replied, "I'm not sure how I feel about the entire situation. I need some time to think about it."

"Well don't think too long," she answered, directly meeting her gaze. "Darnell doesn't seem like the type of man who's going to just sit around and wait for you to make up your mind. You either want it or you don't, but once you decide there's no turning back."

Her pulse quickened. That's what scared her.

Chapter Six

"Ooh, look Mommy!" Chance cried as he held up another item for her to see.

L iberty smiled. "Wow! That's nice." *He already had two dump trucks.*

She glanced down at her watch then rolled her eyes to the ceiling. She would have to remember to strangle Cash the next time she saw her. She had given him a gift card for helping her clean her storage room last weekend. His godmother was always finding an excuse to spoil Chance.

Next time she can take him to the toy store.

Christmas carols were playing and the toy store was like a winter wonderland. Three weeks before Christmas. Kids were screeching and running around. The checkout lines were clear back in the aisle. The only reason why she had come out this evening was because Chance had been begging to speak with Santa Claus. She had seen on the news he was at the store so she had come out in the cold so Chance would have a chance to give Santa his list. They had stood in line for almost an hour. Five minutes and twenty-dollars-worth of instant Polaroid's later, Chance was running around the store eyeballing everything on the shelves.

Liberty followed Chance as he raced from one aisle to the next. Every toy was better than the last he picked up. At some point she was going to have to put her foot down and insist he pick something or leave the store with nothing.

Her phone vibrated in her purse and she reached inside. It was her assistant manager, who made it possible for her to go home most evenings.

"Hey Tiara, what's going on?"

"Beverly called out. Car trouble."

"Dammit," she muttered under her breath. Beverly had a yoga class scheduled to begin in an hour. "Let me see if I can get Cash to teach it, otherwise I will be in. Is the nursery busy tonight?"

"Yes, I can see Colby in there running around the room with the kids."

Her words caused Liberty to grin. At least something was going right. Ms. Dawson had the night off so Chance was just going to have to join them. "Hold off on cancelling the class. Let me try Cash and one of us will call you back."

As soon as she ended the call Liberty reached down to dial Cash's number and as she waited for her to answer, she looked over and noticed Chance was no longer playing with the dump trucks. She took the phone from her ear and glanced up and down the aisle. It wasn't until she called his name and he didn't answer that she started to panic. With her heels clicking rapidly across the concrete floor she hurried over to the next aisle.

"Liberty, you there?"

She had forgotten she had called Cash. "I'm going to have to call you back. Thanks to you I am at the toy store and now I can't find Chance," she said frantically as she raced up the aisle.

"Check the train! That's his hang-out spot. It's at the back of the store near the restrooms."

"Okay. Thanks," she breathed and hurried toward the rear. "Oh! Can you call the gym? We need a yoga teacher tonight."

"Sure, I'll cancel my date and go handle it. Now go find my godson... and call me back!"

Liberty ended the call and hurried around the corner toward the sound of a train chugging along a track, and who she saw, caused her to heart rate to increase.

Darnell.

The second their eyes met her body came to life. Goodness, he was delicious. From the close-cropped hair to the rock-hard body in a dark suit and white shirt that couldn't be disguised beneath a long black trench coat.

"I think I have something that belongs to you," he murmured. There was that wicked voice that sent shivers down her spine.

"Yes you do." She walked toward him and felt a tug at the pit of her stomach. "Thank you," she said and immediately scooped her son up into her arms and squeezed him tight. "Don't you ever run off like that ever again! You scared me," she said in a gentle tone.

"Sorry Mommy," he said with a long face and she quickly dropped kisses along his lips and cheeks. Chance squirmed and giggled then drew back and pointed at the man beside her that she was trying to ignore. "Mommy look! It's my friend. Remember?"

How in the world could she forget? Liberty tried to resist looking into his eyes, but once his stare caught it was hard to look away.

She cleared her throat. "Say hello to Mr. Darnell."

"Call me Mr. Dee." Darnell looked at her for approval, then shrugged. "It's easier."

"Hi Mr. Dee," Chance repeated and squirmed for her to put him down. As soon as she lowered him to the floor, he dashed over to stand with the other kids and watched the train travel down the monstrous track.

"I looked away for a second and he ran off." She felt the need to explain. The last thing she needed was for him to think she was a bad mother.

Darnell nodded, his eyes never leaving hers. "Boys are sneaky little rascals."

She gave a nervous laugh and noticed his jaw dark with the beginning of stubble.

. "How are you?" he said then licked his lips and her insides tightened. Her focus was zeroed in on him.

"I'm fine," she replied and Chance raced over again and tapped his new friend on the thigh.

"Mr. Dee, you like the Power Rangers?"

He released her from his gaze long enough to grin down at her son. "I do. Leonardo is my favorite."

"Me too!" Chance squealed.

Darnell patted him affectionately on his head and Liberty felt her stomach turn over. Chance dashed back over to the train. Darnell's eyes returned slowly to her face and she found herself once again trapped in the smoldering heat of his gaze.

"What are you doing in a toy store?" she asked trying to shake the spell.

"I'm a big kid at heart," he replied with a sheepish grin. "Actually, I'm shopping for a birthday present for my nephew. That poor kid was born ten days before Christmas."

"December is double the fun for him."

"Not really. Instead of getting him two gifts for Christmas. I give him one for his birthday and another for the holiday. He doesn't know it yet but he's been cheated all his life." Beneath the expensive suit he wore, his chest rose and fell with laughter. Liberty couldn't resist a chuckle of her own.

"That's my little man though," he said and she could see the affection he had for his nephew in his eyes.

"Do you have any other nieces and nephews?" she asked softly.

"Not yet. So between all of us, JJ is spoiled rotten. Especially my father. He enjoys being a grandfather."

She smiled. "I can imagine."

There was another long silence as his eyes drifted over to where Chance was playing with another little boy. *That's what it would be like for Chance to have a cousin.* Something he'd never had.

"I spoke to an attorney."

Her shoulders stiffened. "So you're really going through with this?" she said as anger swelled inside her chest. Liberty wanted to scream at the top of her lungs if they hadn't been in a public place. When she took a step back, Darnell reached out and grabbed her hand, sending an unwanted shrill of pleasure through her.

"Liberty please let me finish. I spoke to an attorney just to get his opinion, that's all." He searched her eyes that were blazing up at him. "I want to be in my son's life, Liberty. And after talking to him, I decided I would much rather the two of us work out something together without getting lawyers and courts involved."

Possessiveness gripped her heart and even after his response, she still felt the urge to lash back at him and storm out the store with her son, but she knew that wasn't the answer. Darnell was right. The last thing she needed was months of battling in court when the two of them seemed reasonable enough to be able to maybe work out some kind of arrangement together.

Keep your enemies closer.

Liberty finally said with a stubborn tilt of her chin,

"I'm willing to talk about it."

"Thank you. I appreciate that," Darnell replied, with this overly confident smile that caused her pulse to race. "I'd like to start by giving you a chance to get to know me. If you find out you don't like what you see then I will back off."

She gave him a suspicious look. She was smart enough to know it simply couldn't be that easy. But as their gazes locked the air between them crackled. What in the world was going on? "Sure ... Okay."

He looked pleased by her answer. "How about having dinner with me this Friday night?"

She was stunned. "Dinner? Are you serious?"

"Yes, dinner," he urged. "How's eight o'clock?"

Her pulse raced with something she couldn't quite put her finger on. Darnell was dangerous. But it wasn't fear, no it was slow, pulsing and purely sexual. She wrestled with his proposal for a second, her mind racing through the pros and cons. Part of her wanted to throw his dinner invitation back in his face, but the other part of her wanted to keep him close long enough to figure out what his intentions were.

Holding her gaze, he brought her hand to his lips. "C'mon Liberty. It's a simple answer. Dinner, you and I in a public place." His lip quirked with amusement.

Was he teasing her? She was having a hard time concentrating with his warm full lips on her skin. *Goodness, why did he have to be sexy as hell!*

Heat pooled between her legs, and Liberty wasn't sure how long she stood there before she drew a shaky breath and said, "Okay."

♥ ♥ ♥

Before Darnell even had a chance to discuss the specifics, Liberty took Chance's hand and spun around sending her wild spiral brown hair whipping as she moved through the store. She was wearing dark black slacks and a gray sweater that clung to her large breasts that he didn't miss beneath a short leather jacket. He watched as she sauntered off, her sweet back-side swaying with each step.

She wasn't the only one surprised by the dinner invitation, hell, he surprised himself. But the longer he stood there staring at the two of them, the more he knew that there was no way in hell he was backing down now. As Dax had pointed out, being in his son's life, meant winning over his mother with his irresistible charm. Without a court battle that was the only way that was going to be possible.

Darnell caught up with her in a few short strides. He noticed the way her eyes widened slightly at his nearness. Good. At least he wasn't the only one affected.

"Hey! Chance dropped this," he said as he held out the small knit glove to match the one he was wearing.

She hesitated, almost as if afraid to take it from his hand before she reached out to retrieve it and when she did their fingers brushed and he felt heat radiate up his arm.

"Thanks," she said in a shaky breath.

"I'll call you later. You gonna be at the gym?" he asked.

She nodded. "I might have to teach a class tonight."

"Class?" His lips quirked. "You're an aerobics instructor too?"

She gave a low sexy chuckle that he felt right smack at the groin. "Yes. I might own the club, but I started out teaching step aerobics."

"I can't wait to see you in action," he said with a teasing smile.

Her beautiful eyes widened with alarm. "You wouldn't dare!"

"Maybe not tonight, but I will." He winked. "I'll call you later."

Chapter Seven

"Hold still!" Cash barked as she ran the brush through Liberty's hair.

Liberty blew out a breath as she glared at her best friend through the vanity mirror. Cash could be so bossy. "How much longer is this going to take?"

"Just a few more minutes. Relax."

How in the world was she supposed to relax? She had a date tonight with a gorgeous man who was also the father of her child. "I would rather wear my hair the same way I do every day."

Cash gave a rude snort and waved the blue flat iron in the air. "Absolutely not. It's a hot mess! I don't know why you don't go to the beauty shop and let them get rid of the frizz in your hair."

"I told you I don't want chemicals in my hair. That's the whole reason for natural hair." Liberty slumped back against the chair and pouted.

"Yes, but natural hair requires regular maintenance and you suck at that, which is why I am over at your house doing your hair."

"You're over here because you're my babysitter."

"Yep. That too," she laughed and raked the comb through her hair and hit a tangle.

"Ouch!" Liberty cried.

Maybe Cash was right. But she loved her hair natural. She had stopped putting chemicals in her hair five years ago and never regretted it. Most days she just went wild and wavy doing nothing more than running her fingers through her curls before walking out the door. However when it was a special occasion—or so Cash thought—she allowed her best friend to come over, armed and dangerous, with her flat iron.

"What did Lee say when you cancelled your date with him tonight?"

Liberty rolled her eyes at the question. The conversation hadn't gone well at all. "At first he was quiet, but then he started asking a million questions. What am I doing? Was it with another man? I told him it was a private matter and then he started going on and on about how much money he had invested in me."

"You're lying!" she shrieked.

Liberty shook her head. "No, I'm afraid I'm not. I was so shocked by the way he reacted, I asked him never to call me again."

Cash smirked at her reflection. "You should have told him *Daddy's home.*"

Liberty met her gaze and the two burst out in laughter.

"I'm just glad you found out he was crazy now than later," Cash chuckled.

So am I. Every time she found a man who she thought had potential, something always went wrong. Why's that? she wondered.

"As soon as I get done with your hair, I want to see this outfit you're planning on wearing."

Liberty looked up at her skeptical expression. "Why? You don't trust me?"

"Absolutely not. All you mothers forget how to reel in a man. But I'm here to help you bring sexy back."

79

"Why? It's not really a date," Liberty argued, but it seemed the only person she was trying to convince was herself. It was apparent by Cash's face she didn't believe a word of it.

"Yeah, right."

Liberty drew a deep breath. She would never admit the date had been the only thing she could think about ever since they had met at the toy store.

She should hate Darnell for barging into her life with his demands and yet there was something so arousing about the man that if she wasn't careful Darnell might manage to persuade her to do a lot more than just allow him to spend time with his son.

His son.

It was still hard for her to believe and until she was completely certain, she just didn't want to talk it into existence. The only good thing about it was Chance would grow up knowing his father. What role Darnell would play in his life remained to be seen, but until she got a chance to really know him and his intentions, there was no way in hell she was allowing him to be in her son's life.

By the time she heard a vehicle pull in front of the house, her knees were shaking.

"You look gorgeous," Cash said standing in her bedroom door admiring her own handiwork. "I'll go down and let him in." With one final look, she departed to answer the door.

Liberty swung side-to-side in front of the door-length mirror. Leave it to her best friend to make sure that she not only looked good but that she felt beautiful as well.

She was wearing a long gray sweater dress that engulfed her curves to perfection. A belt accentuated her small waist and knee-high burgundy suede boots complemented the look. Her hair was straight and swinging loose around her shoulders. Makeup was minimal and yet it was just enough to bring out her eyes and define her high cheekbones. As she took a final look, her brow bunched with concern. The last thing she wanted was for Darnell to think she had gone to all this trouble for him even though in all honesty she had.

Let him think whatever he wants, she finally decided with a smirk.

By the time Liberty made it down the stairs into the living room, Chance was showing his remote control car to Darnell. The second Darnell looked up their eyes connected and her heart jumped in her chest. It was brief but just long enough to cause her body to start to heat again.

How was she supposed to spend the evening with him?

He looked gorgeous and relaxed in dark blue jeans and a black pullover sweater beneath a leather bomber jacket. On his feet were black Polo boots. Darnell was kneeling on the floor and now had the remote control in his hand. Chance was standing beside him, eyes wide with excitement as he watched the toy sports car zip up and down the length of the room.

While she watched them, she stood there thinking, *we created this child together*. Maybe not in the normal sense but still Chance had been created by them. And the thought was so strong it sent heat raging in areas it didn't need to be.

At that moment, Darnell looked over and again their eyes locked, only this time the pull was so powerful, she couldn't look away nor did she have the strength to breathe.

'The car crashed into the coffee table, breaking the

spell. Liberty took several deep breaths as she watched Darnell stand, drawing her eyes to the powerful muscles beneath the cashmere sweater before lowering to her son who was crawling around on the floor.

"Thanks for letting me drive your car," Darnell said, voice deep and husky as he handed over the remote.

"You wanna see my room?" Chance asked, while gazing up at him adoringly. He looked so cute, her heart flipped beneath her breasts.

"Chance, let's go have some ice cream," Cash suggested as she peeked her head in from the hall.

"Oh boy!" he squealed then skipped off toward the kitchen with Cash behind him, leaving the two of them alone.

Liberty sauntered into the room, while she tried to concentrate on making her heart slow down.

Darnell lowered his thick lashes and took in her appearance carefully, as if he was mentally stripping off her clothes. "You look lovely," he said, admiring her with hungry eyes.

She blinked. "Thank you," Was all she could come up with. She was at a loss for words.

"You ready to go?" he asked.

She nodded and walked to the coat closet in the hall and removed a black peacoat. Before she could slip her arms inside Darnell came up behind her, took the coat from her hands. She slid her arms inside and could feel the heat of his body behind her as he helped drag it over her shoulders and then adjusted her collar. His warm fingers brushed the hairs at the nape of her neck, sending tingles to all the wrong places.

Liberty immediately gave herself a swift talking to. *This is not a date,* she chanted. They were going to talk about Chance, nothing more.

When he finally stepped away, Liberty looked over her shoulder at him and smiled. "Thank you."

"You're welcome," he replied. She wasn't sure how long she stared at him before he finally moved to the door and opened it.

Get it together. Liberty shook off the effect, reached for her purse on the table in the foyer, and followed Darnell down the stairs and out to his Range Rover. There was snow on the ground and the air was cold enough that she pulled her collar up around her ears. He opened the door for her and made sure the seatbelt was in place before he moved around to the driver's side. As soon as he pulled away from the house, Liberty asked, "Where are you taking me?"

"I was thinking dinner and dancing."

Surprised, she turned on the seat. "Dancing?"

Darnell gave her a devilish grin. "Yes. Dancing. I want to know if my son's mother has rhythm."

She couldn't resist a laugh. "I've got lots of rhythm."

"The jury is still out on that one," he replied with a wink.

As she laughed, Liberty felt some of the tension drain from of her body. "You're talking about me ... What about you?"

"Woman, I taught Chris Brown everything he knows."

Her brow rose with disbelief and he roared with laughter. The sound was so infectious Liberty couldn't resist another snicker of her own. Darnell definitely had a sense of humor, she thought as she took a moment to admire his chiseled jaw that was smothered by a sexy short beard. The man was just too handsome for his own good.

She noticed he was headed to Rehoboth Beach. She

loved going down with Cash and hanging out at the outlet malls. Afterwards they usually stopped for some of the best fish on the east coast.

"Do you like seafood?"

His voice turned her from staring out her window. "I love seafood."

"Good." Darnell nodded and looked pleased by her answer. "I want to take you to this little spot I found close to the shore. They have the best lobster bisque I have ever eaten."

She gave a look of skepticism. "This I gotta taste."

After a few moments of chitchatting, with Darnell asking about her fitness center, Darnell pulled into the crowded parking lot of a restaurant that was right on the ocean. Liberty waited for him to come around and open the door for her before she took his hand and climbed out. The contact caused her heart to trip in a nervous rhythm beneath her breasts. The way his eyes widened was proof he had felt it also.

Soft snow was coming down again and Christmas lights twinkled up and down the retail district. Even during the winter, Rehoboth Beach was a popular place to hang out after dark with places to party, shop and eat.

The scent of fish smelled promising as they headed up a long wooden ramp. Liberty walked beside him toward what looked like a restaurant on water with large picturesque windows, a wrought iron railing leading up to a double red door, and a patio which she was sure was popular when weather permitted.

They stepped inside and she found Fishermen's Cove was packed. The gleaming mahogany bar was lined with patrons and there didn't seem to be an empty table in the room.

A young perky hostess walked up to the podium.

"Welcome! Are you dining in or just here for drinks?"

"Dining in. Simmons ... reservation for two." Darnell came up behind Liberty and placed a hand at her waist. She stilled and had to resist the urge to close her eyes and lean back against his rock-hard chest while the hostess scanned the list of names.

"Simmons...Simmons..., yes, here you are. Your table should be ready shortly."

He nodded and drew Liberty closer to his side so another couple could check in. She took a deep breath and tried to focus her attention on a brightly lit Christmas tree in the corner.

"It smells great in here," she said desperate for something to say.

Darnell leaned down until his lips brushed the side of her ear. "Wait 'til you taste the food." His warm baritone voice sent a gush of heat right smack to her abdomen.

"I can't wait." She laughed and eased away slightly from his touch. She couldn't think with him so close.

A server finally approached them. "Please, follow me."

His hand was still at the small of her back as she guided them to the rear of the restaurant to a linen covered table that was set in front of a large window. Darnell pulled out a chair for her and waited until Liberty was seated before moving around to sit across from her.

The server waited until they were both situated then placed the menus on the table in front of them. "Enjoy your meal."

Smiling, Liberty glanced out the wide window at the boats docked along the harbor. Snow was still falling. Her eyes traveled around the restaurant with exposed beams and an interior that resembled a fisherman's boat. An anchor was on the wall as well as several life rafts suspended from the ceiling.

"What do you think?" Darnell asked while staring at her from across the table.

There was soft music playing in the background. An open fire was crackling from a floor-to-ceiling fireplace to the far right. The restaurant was warm and inviting with dimly lit chandeliers casting a romantic ambiance. She finally nodded and replied, "I've never been here before. It's very nice."

"I found this place by accident one evening," he began, eyes sparkling with amusement. "I had reservations at another restaurant that wouldn't show up on my GPS, so after one wrong turn too many I found myself in this parking lot, hungry as hell, so I decided to give the food a try."

The server came by and filled their water glasses, then moved to the next table.

"What do you recommend?" Liberty asked as she reached for her glass.

Darnell looked up from the menu and when his tongue slipped out to lick his lips a wicked high jolt of electricity surged through her body. "Definitely the bisque. And if you like salmon you can't go wrong."

"Then how about you order for us?" she suggested breathlessly.

"I can do that." His smile rested on her, and Liberty felt her eyes being drawn to his lips. "You drink wine?"

Liberty nodded. "I do." Although she needed to keep a level head. Despite how attracted she was to Darnell, she didn't trust him quite yet.

She returned her gaze to her menu. Anything to keep from looking at him. The mere sight of him, shredded her equilibrium and turned her brain to mush.

Their waitress arrived and Liberty listened as Darnell ordered them a glass of white wine, an order of calamari, and each a bowl of the lobster bisque.

"I rarely eat appetizers," she said conversationally. "I'm going to be full before we get to the main course."

Darnell leaned over the table, grinning at her. "Don't worry. I'll help you eat it."

His words caused a raging inferno inside her stomach.

A bottle of Chardonnay was delivered to the table and Darnell poured each of them a glass then lifted his in the air. "Here's to a new beginning."

Liberty met his gaze from across the table then raised her glass and touched it against his. "New beginnings."

She brought the glass to her lips. The way he was staring had Liberty's body humming with pleasure.

"So ask me a question."

"Excuse me?" Her brow rose at the soft smile curving his sensual mouth.

"I consider this dinner an audition," he said simply. "So ask me a question. Go ahead. I know you're dying to."

"Okay," she said, took a sip then lowered her glass. "Did you make it a habit… donating to a sperm bank?'

He appeared amused by her question. "You get right to it, don't you?"

Liberty shrugged and relaxed on the seat. "Why waste time?"

"I agree," Darnell commented between sips. "To be honest that was the only time I ever went to a bank."

"Really?"

He grinned and was nodding his head at her. "I was attending law school and needed a way to make some quick cash so my roommate suggested going down. Apparently he was a regular donor. Once was enough for me."

She paused for a moment. "Why just once? Why didn't you ever go back?"

"Well, for one I didn't get off on the whole self-gratification process," he said with a chuckle. "Now if I had a beautiful woman like you helping a brotha out, it might have made the process a little more enjoyable."

She giggled along with him and then he quickly sobered and his jaw tightened.

"In all seriousness, I never really thought about my sperm actually creating a life, because if I had, I never would have done it."

"Why's that?" she urged, giving him her undivided attention.

"Because I'm all about family." He took another sip then appeared to be collecting his thoughts before continuing. "After my mother died of a brain aneurysm, my father raised my sister, brother and I alone."

"I'm sorry to hear that."

He shrugged it off. "Thank you. It was a long time ago but I still remember how hard it was for all of us, especially my sister growing up without a mother. My father tried to raise us the best way he could. He's a good man. Worked thirty years as a school bus driver."

She nodded knowingly. "My father raised me after my mother died."

His eyes widened. "So you definitely understand."

"I do." But unlike him, her father never let her forget how much he resented losing his wife in child birth. She blew out a long breath and tried to keep her bottom lip from trembling at the memory.

"My family and I are close, real close," he

explained. "Family means a lot to me so there's no way I could know I have a son and not be a part of his life."

Liberty's skin got all tingly. Every time Darnell spoke about *their* son and how much he wanted to be a part of his life, she got a warm feeling at the center of her chest. Truth was, she had always dreamed of having a man in her life who'd love Chance as much as she did. "Do you have any children?" she asked as she reached for her wine and took another sip.

Darnell saw the look in her eyes. She was testing him. "Other than Chance, no, at least none I know about." He was very careful always using condoms and making sure he personally disposed of them himself. "But I would react the same way I'd reacted when I found out about Chance."

"Do you ever plan on marrying and having a family?"

He answered without hesitation. "Nope. I've never been interested. I'm a divorce attorney and I see the way people change. All the fighting. The kids being torn apart by all the hatred," he said between sips. "Nah, there's no way I'm going through that."

"But all marriages aren't like that," Liberty debated and there was this far off look in her eyes.

Darnell studied her over the rim of his glass. He was sure she was thinking about her husband and yet he felt an unfamiliar wave of longing he just couldn't understand especially when the last thing he wanted was a wife or a family. Well, at least that's what he thought before he found out he had a son. Now the idea of sharing his life with Chance was all he thought about. He was still amazed how quickly his heart had changed over the idea. Was it possible for him to someday change his mind about marriage as well? Darnell scowled at that idea. "True, but I'm not willing to take that chance."

Her lips pursed with disappointment. The waitress arrived with their bisque and he was glad for the interruption. Marriage was just not something he wanted to talk about. "Go ahead," he urged. "Try it."

Liberty brought the spoon to her lips and her eyes fluttered closed. "Oh my... this is delicious."

The soft, husky whimper sent an erotic wave of heat rushing straight to his groin. "I told you," he said watching her every move. He couldn't take his eyes off of her. Liberty's wild hair had been tamed and now brushed hypnotically back and forth along her shoulder blades. One side was swept back and tucked behind her ear. Only he preferred it spiraled and wild and he craved to run his long fingers through it. And then there was that sexy beauty mark right above her upper lip that reminded him of that famous movie star that kept his cock throbbing. If watching her mouth move as she talked wasn't enough, then eating was pure torture. The way her full lips parted and the swipe of her pink tongue each time it slipped out to capture a drizzle of cream from the corner of her mouth was enough to bring him to his knees. Just thinking about what he could do with those lips made it almost impossible to breath.

Liberty caught him staring. "Aren't you going to eat yours?" she said innocently. The woman had no idea how sexy she looked sitting across the table.

Darnell reached for his spoon and while he ate he continued to watch her. There was something special about Liberty he just hadn't quite put his finger on. But one thing for sure she was different from any other woman he'd dated. Not that this was a real date. But the way she had his body reacting, as soon as the evening was over he was going to have to contact one of the chicks he had on speed dial to help relieve the pent-up sexual frustration he'd felt ever since he first laid eyes on Liberty.

"When would you like to get a blood test?" she asked.

Her question was the bucket of cold water he needed. He took a sip before answering. "The sooner the better."

"I agree." She nodded. "The sooner we know if he's your son the better."

Darnell gave a harsh laugh. "Liberty, he's my son." She might be in denial but he wasn't. "You know and I know Chance is mine."

She took another sip of her bisque, then replied, "You're right. There is really little doubt in my mind." She was staring down into her bowl, avoiding eye contact.

"So then why the long face?" he asked between sips.

Liberty brought the napkin from her lap, wiped her mouth, then released a long breath before meeting his eyes head-on. "Because Chance is all I have. A selfish part of me doesn't want to share him."

He studied her, seeing the fear in her eyes and felt the overwhelming need to drag Liberty into his arms and reassure her his intentions weren't malicious. Lowering his spoon, he rested his elbows on the table and stared at her as he said softly, "Liberty I don't want to take him away from you. From what I can see, you are a good mother and doing one helluva job with him."

"Thank you for that." Her shoulders sagged with relief. She blinked and he could tell she was fighting back tears.

Reaching across the table, he comfortably covered

her warm, slender hand with his. "But a boy needs a father, Lib, and I want to be a part of my son's life."

There was a shy smile on her face as she said softly, "I know. And that's hard for me. For four years I was under the impression that I was going to be a single parent raising a son. My husband was never a part of that picture." She shrugged. "I guess after Greg died I just prepared myself for a life alone."

Darnell waited until a dish with crisp calamari was delivered to their table before continuing their discussion.

"I know you said it's none of my business but I still want to know how you ended up with my sperm?"

Liberty took another sip and he could tell she was stalling. Darnell resumed eating his soup while allowing her to take as much time as she needed.

"My husband had a biking accident as a child and as a result he was unable to have children." She put her spoon down and drew a long breath. "He knew how badly I wanted a baby, so he agreed to artificial insemination." While Darnell finished his bisque, Liberty told him about the months of hoping and the miscarriages that followed with more heartache. And as he watched her face, he could see the pain and yearning to have a baby. "I was so excited when I found out I was pregnant with Chance. It was so hard not to tell Greg, but I wanted to make sure it was really going to happen this time." She reached for her water and took another long swallow.

"You said he never found out about Chance?" he asked encouraging her to continue.

She took another drink then replied, "It was going to be his birthday surprise, but he died of a heart attack before I could tell him."

Darnell stilled. "I'm sorry."

She dropped her head to try and disguise the pain before looking across the table again with a smile that seemed forced. "It's been five years. I've got a wonderful little boy, the gym, and my best friend to fill the gap in my life."

"Fill the gap? Are you saying you haven't started dating again?"

She shook her head. "No. I date, but I always know how it's going to end."

He speared a piece of calamari and said, "Sounds to me like you've been dating the wrong men."

She gave a sexy smirk. "Maybe so or maybe I'm just not interested in sharing my life with anyone other than my son."

His brow quirked. "You know that isn't healthy for him or for you."

There was a look of despair as she lowered her spoon. "I know. Cash tells me all the time I'm too overly protective and I'm going to have a mama's boy."

"Oh hell no! No mama's boy," he chuckled. "That's what a father is for... to teach his son how to be a man." He reached over and touched her hand again. "Let me help you with that."

She looked over at him with so much uncertainty he brought her hand to his lips and kissed her fingertips.

Liberty was beautiful, sexy, and the mother of his child, and because she was an important part of his son's life that made her important as well. Only what he was feeling wasn't friendly, instead it was erotic and sexual in nature.

"I'm willing to try," she finally said.

"And that's all that I ask."

♥ ♥ ♥

What in the world is wrong with me? Liberty asked herself as the heat from his hand sent fire zipping to every corner of her body. Allowing Darnell to be in Chance's life was the right decision. Liberty felt it in her heart although she wasn't quite ready to allow him to be alone with her son yet. The problem was how in the world was she going to continue to be around a man who excited her body beyond explanation?

Darnell finally released her hand and she didn't miss the cocky grin on his face.

"Try the calamari," he suggested as he stabbed one with his fork and brought it to her mouth. "Here, open up."

She looked up into his deep penetrating eyes and inhaled sharply before parting her lips and taking a bite.

"Mmmm, that's tender," she managed between chews.

He nodded and finished the remainder on his fork. She blushed and was amazed at how Darnell had no qualms about eating after her. "I told you the food here is worth the drive."

"I see." She reached for her fork and speared another.

The rest of the food was even better. Salmon, oysters dressing and steamed mixed vegetables. They talked and laughed like they had known each other for years, instead of days. Darnell was easy to talk to and Liberty caught herself relaxing on the seat and sharing tidbits of her life growing up in Illinois while Darnell talked about law school. They found out they both hung out at the same coffee shop, and he had rented an apartment in the same building she used to live in with her roommates.

By the time Darnell had paid the check, Liberty was actually looking forward to going dancing.

Darnell took her hand again and helped her into his Range Rover and they listened to the soulful sounds of Kem on the drive back. The whole time she was thinking about dinner, their conversation and Darnell. What was it about him that excited her so much? She didn't want to be interested but she just couldn't seem to help herself.

"I gotta tell you. My dad is anxious to see Chance again."

She snapped her finger. "That was him and your stepmother I saw in the grocery store that day."

He grinned. "That's how I found out about you."

She nodded in remembrance. "I remember your father asking me, 'Is that Dee's son?'"

His eyebrows winged up. "And what did you tell him?"

"I told him I didn't know anyone name Dee," she replied with a laugh.

"It's a small world."

She looked over and grinned. "Yes it is."

Chapter Eight

Darnell took Liberty's hand and led her to the door. The heavy thump of music already had him bobbing his head to the tune. Upscale was the hottest thirty-plus club in Delaware and he would know. He and his cousins made it their mission to patronize every last one from here to Philadelphia and beyond.

"Wow! It's packed," Liberty said as she hurried to keep up with his wide strides.

He slowed and grinned down at her beautiful face, noticing her eyes had widened with excitement. "When was the last time you've been dancing?" he asked curiously.

Her brow rose. "Not since Chance was born."

"What?" he said incredulously. He couldn't imagine not hitting the town every Friday and Saturday night. It was what being single was all about. Doing what you wanted. When you wanted. The only difference now was he had a one-drink limit that he swore by.

"You'll like this place. It's grown folks business."

"I like the sound of that." Liberty giggled and the sound was so compelling, it caused his stomach to do a slow roll.

They flashed their IDs and Darnell took her hand again and made his way across the crowded night club. He saw the excitement dancing in her eyes. He knew that look. He also felt it, and was excited about the night ahead. The plush décor was upscale, contemporary and classy. The music was bumping and everyone seemed to be having a good time. Dozens of small round tables were all occupied with men and women sipping drinks, laughing and socializing. As they settled at a table he'd reserved on one of the elevated platforms, his eyes traveled around the room. It was crowded, and yet the night was still young. A waitress maneuvered her way through the crowd balancing a tray of fruity-looking drinks.

"Would you like anything to drink?" he asked as Liberty shrugged out of her coat.

Smiling, she swung around and Darnell stared at the beautiful woman sitting beside him.

"I'll have whatever you're drinking."

He held up his hands, palms forward. "I've already reached my limit."

She coughed out an incredulous laugh. "Are you serious? One glass of wine?"

He nodded and there was something in her eyes that made him feel compelled to share something he rarely disclosed to anyone. "I spent too many years partying and drinking way too much." He leaned in close so she could hear him over the beat of the music. "A year ago some of my boys and I met in Vegas for the weekend, partying, women, you name it, we were doing it. Anyway we had left this club about three in the morning and my boy Clayton was staying at this time share that wasn't on the strip." He swallowed as the memories came rushing back. "He picked up his car from the valet and got about a mile up the road when he hit a truck head-on and was killed instantly." He saw her eyes widen with alarm. "I should have taken his keys from him or insisted he stayed and slept it off in my suite." Darnell drew a deep breath. "Ever since, I rarely touch the stuff anymore. Beer... wine maybe, but no longer the hard stuff."

Liberty brought a comforting hand to his arm. "I'm so sorry about your friend."

He shrugged. The last thing he wanted was for her to feel sorry for him, but he appreciated the compassion.

"How about a cola with extra ice?" she said with a wink.

"Coming right up," he replied then signaled for a waitress.

♥ ♥ ♥

They had been sitting at their table laughing and talking when Darnell rose from his chair. "Dance with me Liberty." His voice was rough and strained.

"Now?" The song was half over.

"Yes, now," Darnell growled and there was something in his eyes that silenced her. She took the hand he held out to her and allowed him to escort her onto the dance floor and into the circle of his arms. With him pressed up against her, she was getting all hot and bothered and the way his breathing had increased, she knew he felt it too.

She desperately needed to say something. "You better not step on my feet."

He tossed his head back with laughter. "You got me confused. I told you I got skills."

Oh, there was no doubt in her mind of that. He pulled her close, snuggly against his chest, and his arms tightened around her.

"I needed an excuse to hold you," he said swaying slightly.

"Why?" she asked following his lead.

"Because I wanted to know how this body felt." He drew back, gazed down at her and then laughed. "Don't look at me that way. I've been waiting all night to hold you in my arms."

She couldn't resist a smile as she fell into step.

The music changed to Dru Hill. "Oh that's my song," she muttered.

"Then alright now." He drew her close so her breasts rested against his chest and they moved together to the beat of the song. Liberty closed her eyes and when Darnell brought his lips down and brushed her ear, she released a sigh.

"You are so beautiful," he said in a husky voice.

"Thank you," she whispered and realized her body was engulfed in his large, protective arms.

Darnell brought his hands to her waist then pulled back. Liberty tilted her head and their eyes locked. A shiver rippled over her skin and her entire body prickled with heat. *There's something happening between us,* she thought as her heart pounded and her mouth went dry. Something dangerous, intense and potent, and yet invigorating. And she was out of her mind because there was no way she was going to allow anything to happen between them. Despite the fact her body yearned for her to let go and give in to the overwhelming feeling.

Liberty closed her eyes and rested her head on his chest again. "You were right," she murmured and quickly changed the subject. "You're a pretty good dancer." His steps were confident with swag.

"So are you, Lib."

Lib? No one ever called her that but her dad and yet when Darnell used her nickname, it sounded so natural it caused her to shudder.

"Are you cold?" he asked, drawing back to stare

down into her eyes.

"A little," she said.

"Then I better hold you tight," he whispered as he dragged her body even closer and there was no denying the instant heat.

Three songs later, Darnell took her hand and they were headed back toward their table when she heard him say, "Oh damn! Here comes trouble."

She followed the direction of his eyes and to her it looked like double trouble. They were so fine, and there wasn't a woman who hadn't noticed. Heads were turning. Women were whispering. And then there were the hungry stares. She couldn't blame them for drooling. As soon as they spotted Darnell, wide grins spread across their identical handsome faces.

"What's up cuz!" the taller one said. Not that the other was much shorter. Six-three… six-five maybe.

"What's going on?" Darnell said and then gave each of them a fist pound. "I want to introduce you to Liberty. Liberty these are my knucklehead cousins."

They grinned and she felt herself blushing. Goodness, had she died and gone to heaven? They were like melted chocolate, with smooth mocha skin. In a single look she knew they had to be related to Darnell. And anyone could tell the two were twins. One had a bald head while the other's hair was cropped close. They both had goatees. The only distinct difference, one had golden brown eyes like Darnell. The other's eyes were midnight black.

"Nice to finally meet you, "one of the cuties drawled with male appreciation. "I'm Dominic but my friends call me Dax."

She shook hands with the gorgeous dark-eyed man and silently appreciated how handsome they all were. Whatever was in their genes they needed to package it, because it was guaranteed to make any woman's pulse race.

"And I'm Patrick. Everybody calls me good-looking." His large hand engulfed her and she caught herself giggling like a little school-girl.

"Pleasure meeting both of you," she heard herself say.

"So... this is Chance's mom," Patrick said with vivid-eyed male appreciation.

Darnell's hand at her waist tightened possessively. "Yes, this is her."

"Damn! Do all baby mamas look like you?" Dax asked with a wicked smile.

Liberty looked from one to the next. "I don't know how to answer that."

"Okay, you two need to behave," Darnell warned and then they roared with laughter.

The twins followed them back to their table, ordered a round of drinks, and laughed and talked about growing up and Liberty caught herself laughing at some of their ridiculous stories.

"Yo, Dee, man, remember that time Uncle Shaun found out we stole that four-wheeler from Ms. Bea's yard." Patrick chuckled.

Darnell gave a rude snort. "Dad made sure I never forgot," he said and then rubbed his butt and the table shrieked again with laughter.

Liberty sipped a cola and rested her elbows on the table while she listened and watched them all. *Is this my son in another twenty-something years?* she wondered. Impressively they were all lawyers, handsome and single. God help the women of Sheraton Beach!

"Don't look now but I think I've spotted my future baby mama." Dax tossed his glass back, finishing his drink with one gulp then excused himself, and maneuvered his way through the crowd.

Patrick lowered the bottle of beer with a thump. "I guess it's time for me to let all these ladies see what they've been missing all their lives." He hustled off and Darnell turned to her, shaking his head.

"You've got to excuse my cousins. They're a handful."

She took a lay sip of her cola and replied, "I see. But I like them."

A smile kicked his lips up and her heart into gear. "And I can see they like you too, but then what's not to like."

He dragged her back onto the dance floor and they bumped and grinded some more. On the way back to the table he excused himself and disappeared in the men's room. Liberty took that moment to take a deep breath and try to get herself together. *What in the world are you doing?* Tonight was supposed to be about getting to know Darnell and finding out if she could trust him. Instead she couldn't think straight with electricity sizzling over every inch of her skin.

At the sound of the electric slide, a crowd of women screamed and flooded the dance floor. Liberty watched, nodding her head to the familiar beat. Out the corner of her eye, she spotted him talking to Dax near the bar. She looked at him, standing there all tall and yummy. *That man has enough charisma and confidence for two men.*

By the next song, Darnell was dragging her back onto the dance floor. Goodness! She knew she should end the evening and ask that he take her back home but she just couldn't do it. It had been a long time since she'd enjoyed herself so much and since it would never happen again she wanted to enjoy every moment for as long as it lasted.

♥ ♥ ♥

"I had a great time tonight."

She climbed out and pulled up her collar against the brisk cold nipping at her cheeks. "So did I." Better than she had ever imagined.

They climbed the stairs and Liberty wasted no time turning the key in the lock. "Come inside where it's warm," she suggested and signaled for Darnell to follow her. He pulled the door closed behind him. It was quiet upstairs so she knew Chance and Cash were asleep.

With his assistance, she slipped out of her coat and then he carried it to the coat closet and hung it up for her.

Such a gentleman.

They were still standing in the foyer. "Would you like something to drink? Hot cocoa?" she offered.

Darnell smiled, but shook his head. "No, I better go."

"Oh, okay." She suddenly realized they were all alone and it was late.

He smiled. "I'd like to take you and Chance bowling on Friday."

Her brow rose with amusement. "Bowling! I am a lousy bowler."

"Don't worry about it," he chuckled. "That's why they have bumpers."

She laughed. Chance would truly enjoy it.

"I'll give you a call tomorrow." His voice curled around her in a hot embrace, making her shiver with want.

She swallowed. "I'd like that."

"Good-night, Lib."

Liberty barely had time to take a breath before

Darnell's mouth came down on hers. *Whoa!* The sensation of his lips pressed against hers felt too incredible to reject. Darnell backed her slowly until her shoulder hit the wall, then he dragged her arms up over her head and kissed her as she'd never been kissed before. Hard, dominate, arousing, and yet so damn hot, sending sparks of something delicious shooting through her system. Following a moan, Liberty parted her lips and his tongue slid into her mouth, sending a jolt of pleasure that caused her knees to buckle slightly. His tongue tangled with hers, tasting her completely and Liberty found herself melting into him, giving in to the incredible feeling.

Darnell tasted of breath mints and hot male wanting as his tongue slid confidently around hers. Greedily, they drank of each other and Liberty angled her head, seeking more and more. The sensation of his lips was unfamiliar and so damn arousing Liberty wanted to cry. Darnell made her feel things she had only dreamed of. His mouth sent pleasure flaring to her abdomen and traveling downward until a hot wave of sensation seized her between her thighs.

He finally released her wrists and his hand moved to her butt, crushing her against the hard muscles of his legs, and there was no avoiding what was throbbing long and hard against his thigh. A whimper caught in her throat. She wanted him to carry her up the stairs to her bedroom and fulfill every fantasy she'd ever had in ways she was certain he knew how.

Fantasy? What am I doing?

With a final nip of his teeth over her swollen lips, Liberty reluctantly pulled away just enough to stare up into his amber gaze. Her stomach did a back flip at the lust burning in his eyes as if he'd known what she had been thinking.

"It's getting late," she barely managed between breaths.

Nodding he leaned in and kissed her lips once more, then he released her. "Good night, Lib."

She stood and watched as he walked out the door. If she didn't know it before, she knew it now. She was in trouble.

♥ ♥ ♥

The entire ride home, Darnell went over every snippet of their date as he tried to get Liberty out of his head. Only she wouldn't go. Instead he kept hearing her soft voice, and seeing the light shining in those big bright eyes and that dazzling smile.

And then there was that kiss.

With a scowl, Darnell dragged a hand through his hair. This was not at all how he had planned the evening to end, or had he?

Dax told him the fastest way to get what he wanted was to win over Liberty by throwing on the sexy Simmons charm. He had planned to reel her in with his signature grin and charisma and he figured by the end of the evening he would have her eating out of his hand. But if that was the case, how the hell did he end up thinking about not only his son but also in ways to spend more time with Liberty?

And that just wasn't possible.

He didn't allow women to consume his mind or body and yet he couldn't get her out of his head, or get a damn hard-on to go away.

Darnell felt his cell phone vibrating in his pocket again. He pulled it out and a picture of a honey he had met two weeks ago appeared on the screen. Tabitha was a red-bone pharmacist who had a few tricks that had his toes curling by the end of the night. She was definitely one woman he planned on seeing again. But instead of answering the call, he hit Decline and tossed the phone onto the seat beside him. After an evening with Liberty he couldn't even stomach the idea of ending the night with someone else.

So much for getting rid of my pent-up sexual frustration. What the hell is wrong with me? he scowled and punched the steering wheel with frustration. He didn't want a relationship or for a woman to become so important she effed up his head. Yet why was the only bed he wanted to share tonight was the one woman who had abruptly ended their kiss and sent him out the door?

Dragging a hand across his head again, Darnell started laughing uncontrollably. There was no way in hell he was *that* attracted to her. No way was he going to stop being the man that he was—a confirmed bachelor. He pushed the unwanted thoughts of a relationship out of his head. He was a divorce attorney. He didn't believe in committed and especially not love and marriage. All he wanted was to get close to his son. *That's it.* Darnell scowled.

Now he just had to find a way to get his body to listen.

Chapter Nine

"If I wanted to spend my lunch hour alone, I wouldn't have bothered to drop by and get you."

Liberty blinked then smiled sheepishly. "Sorry, I had something on my mind."

"Something or someone?" Cash asked with a knowing look.

Liberty blushed and dropped her eyes to her plate.

They were at Clarence's Chicken & Fish House. It was the lunch rush and as usual the place was filled with chatter. Ever since the restaurant had been nominated for a Neighborhood Award by the *Steve Harvey Morning Show*, getting a table was next to impossible so they always ate after the afternoon rush. The concept seemed to work out just fine. For once she didn't hear the laughter or conversations around the room. The only thing she heard was the banging of her own heart.

Why can't I stop thinking about him?

There was a possessiveness about Darnell and an air of power that radiated from the way his body moved, the look in his eyes, and the timbre of his voice. He could easily control her, possess her, hold her captive with a look or the sound of his voice or a touch. She shook her head to scatter her thoughts. *No sense in allowing her imagination to get the best of her.* Their date had been for Chance's sake and nothing more. He was her son's father and that's where it ended. That's where it had to end.

If only she could get her body to listen.

"Are you going to tell me how your date went or not?"

"I told you it was nice."

"Nice?" Cash gave her an incredulous look. "There is nothing *nice* about dating someone that fine. Arousing... dangerous... but not nice."

Liberty shrugged. "I like him."

Her eyes widened. "You like him? Uh-uh. You need to stop playing and give me some details."

"I already told you."

"No, when I came downstairs and asked, you yawned and said dinner was nice and rushed off to bed. If my mother hadn't insisted I drive her to Philadelphia for the weekend to visit my aunt, I would have stood outside your door all night until I got answers."

Liberty giggled, reached for her catfish and took a bite before continuing. "I mean dinner was delicious, the conversation felt so natural, and the kiss..." she purposely allowed her voice to trail off and wasn't at all surprised when Cash started screaming.

"*Oh my God*! He kissed you?" Her eyes were practically bulging out her head.

Liberty's lips tingled just thinking about it. She couldn't find the words so she simply nodded. And there was nothing she'd like better than for him to kiss her again. Just the thought had her sighing.

Cash fanned herself with her hand. "Well I'll be damned. No wonder you're still in a daze. A man that fine, if he kissed me I'd be on life support."

The two exploded with laughter.

She released a slow shaky breath and went back to eating her food. No man had ever made her feel that good. Her lips were still burning, eager for round two.

"When the two of you weren't kissing, did you talk about Chance?"

Liberty nodded and was glad Cash had changed the subject. She didn't need to be thinking about him or his luscious lips. "We're going to take blood tests."

Cash frowned. "Blood test? Anybody can look at that boy and know who his daddy is. It's you that they might question."

Wrinkling her nose, she said, "Whatever. He came out of this womb. You were there, remember?"

"Yeah, I guess I was there." She gave a silly grin, then bit into her fish.

Liberty's expression became serious. "It's me that wants the blood test. Not Darnell. I just need to be completely sure before I allow some stranger to become a part of my son's life."

"I can understand that, even though it's a waste of money."

She grinned and felt like a schoolgirl after her first date as she told her friend everything that had happened on Friday and ended with Darnell picking them up on Saturday afternoon to go bowling. The memory of each of them laughing and taking turns rolling the ball down the lane still warmed her heart. After hitting a burger joint he had taken them home and ended the evening with a single kiss that was far from simple. She spent the rest of the weekend with Darnell on her mind with thoughts of his lips drifting lightly over hers.

Abruptly, Liberty shook the thought away. "He invited us to his nephew's birthday party on Saturday."

"Really? Introducing you to the family already? I'm impressed," Cash said with a saucy grin.

She flushed. "'He wants Chance to meet his family."

"I ain't mad at him!" she managed while shoving a French fry into her mouth.

She would just have to remember that this was about Chance, not her.

Cash smiled gently at her. "So are the two of you now dating?"

"No," Liberty said quickly. "We're just spending time getting to know each other for the sake of Chance."

She shook her head as she chewed. "You don't really believe that, do you?"

"Of course I do," she said with little conviction.

Cash stared at her for along moment, pointing her fork in her direction. "Well, I think you're wrong. If he kissed you the way you said he kissed you then there's more going on between the two of you than you're admitting."

Liberty swallowed and dropped her gaze to her food so Cash couldn't see the yearning in her eyes. She tried to pretend it was just about Chance, but after spending time together on Saturday, she was starting to feel that there really was a lot more going on than she would allow herself to admit. There was no denying she felt a connection with Darnell that was far more than sharing a child. There was a nagging desire to become more to Darnell than just his son's mother. *Why? Why now?* She kept asking herself. After all of the men she had dated, why did she have to be attracted to someone who had made it clear he wasn't interested in marriage? While she took another bite of her fish, Liberty tried to focus on all the reasons why falling for Darnell would be a terrible mistake. But yet, how could she resist a man who was smart, funny, and downright sexy? And most importantly, he was passionate about being a father. It was crazy but even though he said he wasn't interested in a relationship, deep down a part of her hoped Cash was right and eventually Darnell changed his mind. But until he gave her some kind of clue he wanted more, she was going to have to remember to keep her guard up, because the last thing she needed in her life was another heartbreak.

While they finished their lunch, Cash talked about the babies in the neonatal unit where she worked. Liberty commended her for her dedication. There was no way she could have worked around sick infants all the time and not fall apart. Cash had known when she first decided to become a nurse she wanted to work in a unit where she felt like she was making a difference. Teaching yoga twice a week at the gym was her way of unleashing her frustrations.

"Hey before we head back, I wanna show you this dress at Jennie's Couture." Cash said after she tossed a tip onto the table.

"Okay." Nodding, Liberty buttoned her red peacoat and then slid her hands into the black leather gloves as they headed to the door.

"I want you to see this pink leather bag I saw in the window. It's been calling my name," Cash explained and Liberty couldn't miss the excitement in her voice. Her best friend was a true shopaholic.

Liberty fell into step beside her, snow crunching underneath her booted feet on the sidewalk. Her eyes traveled up and down the wide cobblestone streets that were lined with single story buildings and mom and pop stores. Christmas decorations twinkled in storefront windows, taunting customers to come inside. Holiday wreaths hung on doors and gold tinsel wrapped light posts up and down Main Street.

Customers were everywhere carrying big bags filled with gifts. As always Liberty felt herself being pulled into the festivities. Christmas in Sheraton Beach was one event she looked forward to each and every year.

Cash ended up purchasing the purse. Liberty found a navy blue bag she really liked, but that close to Christmas it was a little out of her price range so she purchased a brown pair of leather gloves instead.

As they were leaving the store, she was laughing at something Cash had said when she looked up the street and her breath caught. Darnell was coming up the sidewalk with long powerful strides. She hated that her heartbeat jumped into her throat at the sight of him moving her way with the grace of a panther. His powerful thighs were encased in dark slacks to match his suit jacket, and he was also wearing a heavy wool coat with a gray scarf around his neck. The entire ensemble screamed expensive.

"Is that who I think it is?" she heard Cash mumble and all Liberty could do was nod.

Panty-dripping handsome, that's what he was. And as those golden-brown eyes drew closer and then sparkled with recognition, Liberty felt cream pooling at her dry crotch. *Damn he was gorgeous!* After several breathtaking moments, Darnell finally reached them and spoke.

"Hello Lib.... and friend."

"Hey, Dee." Liberty struggled to clear her throat as he moved close enough for her to smell the scent of his cologne. "This is ... uh, Cash... Chance's godmother."

She stepped forward. "We met the other day at the house, remember?" Cash gave her a weird look. Goodness, she couldn't think straight when he was around.

"Oh yeah, I forgot about that," Liberty mumbled,

and decided she sounded like an idiot. *Get it together Lib.*

While Cash and Darnell talked, she stood back and tried to ignore the timbre of his voice and the single dimple at his right jaw. But she was shivering and it had nothing to do with the cold air.

"Where are you ladies headed?" he asked and finally returned his gaze to her.

Cash glanced down at her watch. "I've gotta get back to work."

"I'm going back to the gym," Liberty replied.

"I'm on my way to Debbie Cakes on the corner? Walk with me." The power of his intense stare, stole her breath away, and suddenly she panicked.

"Uh..., I can't. She's my ride."

Cash started backing up as she spoke, "Actually, I better get back to the hospital. So you'll need to find another ride."

"Cash!" she gasped at the way her best friend was abandoning her.

A wicked smiled curled Darnell's lips. "I'll make sure she gets home safely."

"Yes, I bet you can," Cash murmured and ignored the outraged look on her best friend's face. "I'll call you later." She blew an air kiss, waved her shopping bag in the air and hurried off to her car.

Traitor.

Darnell gave her a lazy smile. "Well, let's go before we freeze." He offered his arm.

Her stomach quivered as she latched on and fell into step beside him.

"How's your day?" he asked.

With her heart pounding like crazy Liberty wasn't sure how she found the words to speak. "It's been busy at the gym. How about you?"

"I'm just getting out of court. My brother texted and reminded me it's my stepmother's birthday and she loves those red velvet Debbie Cakes." One corner of his mouth lifted and Liberty hated to admit even to herself the impact that small gesture did to her libido.

"I've never been there."

He groaned. "No? Oh man, then sweetheart you are in for a treat!"

Her nipples beaded at the way *sweetheart* rolled off his tongue so naturally. She nodded. "Okay, I can't wait to taste them."

They stepped into the quaint cupcake shop on the corner of Main Street and immediately the smell of cake batter ruffled Liberty's nose. She glanced around at the chic décor. There were several bistro tables and chairs near the large storefront windows with customers sipping coffee, children were drinking hot cocoa while munching on fresh baked cupcakes.

Liberty stepped into line and Darnell moved beside her. His body next to hers and the cologne he was wearing smelled so masculine, she had to fight the urge to lean her head against his chest and inhale.

"I hope you like cupcakes," he said.

Liberty glanced up at him and grinned. "I love them."

Darnell licked his lips and she felt her clit twitched as he growled, "I just bet you do."

With a smile, Liberty shook her head. Darnell was a shameless flirt and so sexy, it was hard to resist his charm. Moving closer to the large display case, Liberty forced her eyes away from the yummy-looking man and focused on the array of delicious treats. She eyed a fudge cupcake and licked her lips, but it didn't look anywhere near as scrumptious as the man standing so close she could have gobbled him up.

While the sales clerk helped a young woman with an assortment of cupcakes, Liberty scanned the selection. "Ooh! I think I might even get the red velvet."

"That's Jennifer's favorite."

"Who?" She turned her head and realized Darnell was leaning in so close, she could have tilted her chin oh so lightly and her lips would have brushed his.

"My stepmother... remember?"

"Oh," she mumbled and then giggled like a school girl. She was having a hard time concentrating with him so close. She tried not to stare but she yearned to feel his mouth on hers, and as she remembered her dream from the previous night, those lips had traveled to a couple of intimate places as well.

"I love it when you laugh."

"You do?" she said sounding breathless.

He nodded and brought a hand to her waist, drawing her closer. "Every time I hear it I can't do anything but smile."

She tried not to stare at his mouth but everywhere her eyes traveled was just as dangerous. His gorgeous eyes... sexy beard... and then to his mouth again. Only this time she couldn't ignore the yearning and found herself meeting his gaze just as he leaned forward and brought his lips down towards—

"Dee, how are you?"

Just before their lips touched, Darnell's head whipped around, breaking the spell. Liberty drew in a shaky breath then took a step back from the glass as a beautiful full-figured woman came from around the counter wearing an apron.

"Hey Debra." Darnell walked over, giving Liberty some much needed space. He gave the woman a big hug then drew back. "How's it going?"

"Good," she replied smiling up at him.

Darnell released her and turned toward Liberty, gazing at her in a way that made her insides turn to mush. "Debra, I'd like you to meet Liberty."

The woman's eyes crinkled warmly as she held out her hand. "Hi Liberty, welcome to my store."

She shook her hand. "It's a pleasure meeting you. It smells wonderful in here."

"Good, then that means there's something in here you like."

"I see several I like." And there was one thing in particular but he wasn't on the menu.

Debbie winked playfully at her. "Then order one of each."

Darnell chuckled. "Lib, it's a good thing you own a gym because you're gonna need it."

"You own a gym, which one?" Debra asked with a curious look.

"*24/7 Fitness,*" Liberty replied and felt herself blushing.

Her eyes lit up with recognition. "Oh I was just telling my fiancé I wanted to check it out."

"Then come on over. We're always looking for new members," Liberty encouraged. "When you do, make sure you ask for me." She fumbled around in her purse and retrieved a business card and handed it to her.

Debbie glanced down at the pink card and smiled. "I'll definitely drop by after the holidays."

"How's Rance doing?" Darnell said, reminding them he was standing there. *As if I could forget.*

Liberty noticed the way Debbie's eyes lit up. "Busy getting ready for the upcoming season, but he'll be down for Christmas."

Darnell pointed his finger at her. "Lib, this woman here snagged Rance Beaumont of the Philadelphia

Sixers."

Liberty's eyes widened. "I remember hearing something about him proposing in front of the entire town."

Debbie blushed. "Something like that."

"Congratulations," Liberty replied and when she spotted the huge rock on her finger, she felt a wave of envy.

"Thank you." Debbie blinked and then rubbed her hands together. "Okay then what can I get you two?"

"I'll take a dozen red velvet in a gift box," Darnell replied then turned to Liberty. "What about you?"

She felt like a child in an ice cream shop. "Hmmm, so many decisions." Liberty decided to go with her favorites. "I'll take one fudge, one red velvet and a coconut." She would share the calories with Chance and Cash.

"Coming right up." Debra moved over to the display holding a decorated cream-colored box and filled it with the red delicious cupcakes.

"Is your stepmother's birthday today?" Liberty asked conversationally.

He flashed a lazy smile and nodded. "Yep. My family is going out to dinner tonight. You wanna come?"

She swallowed hard and drew her gaze to his face, searching his eyes. He'd asked her to walk with him, tried to kiss her, and now invited her to share in an intimate family event. Did he really want her there? There was no denying she loved every moment she spent with him and that was a problem. There was no future with him. Darnell had made it clear in no uncertain terms he wasn't looking for a family and most definitely not a wife. So she'd be setting herself up for heartbreak by allowing herself to get attached.

Shaking her head, she replied, "No, I have a class to teach, but please tell her I said happy birthday."

"No problem."

For a second Liberty thought maybe she had seen a flash of disappointment but it was so brief, there wasn't time to register the possibility, besides, she was certain her mind was playing tricks on her.

♥ ♥ ♥

He couldn't stop looking at her.

Hell, he couldn't stop thinking about her. In his dreams..., while in court. She was threatening the control he had on his life. He'd never let a woman get to him like this. Ever. So why now? Their time together was supposed to be about him getting what he wanted. His son. Not Liberty. Yet why every time he saw her his body got hot and hard?

It was a good thing she had declined his offer because somehow he had to get her out of his head.

But even with that thought in mind, Darnell caught himself watching her out the corner of his eyes, talking merrily with Debra while she tied a big red bow around the box. Liberty was gorgeous in jeans that hugged her lush hips and ass and then there was that gray V-neck sweater. Every time she spoke, her breasts rose and fell with each breath and it took everything he had not to look. But it was next to impossible. He found Liberty sexy and beautiful in so many ways from her hair pulled up in a ponytail, to the lip gloss shimmering on those amazing lips.

All he knew was he had to get her out of his head. A woman consuming his thoughts and body was not what he wanted at all, which was why he didn't do relationships. The problem was figuring out how to stop it.

Liberty giggled and the erotic sound caused his loins to stir again.

I'm going to strangle Dax when I see him.

It had been his lame-brained idea to use the sexy Simmons charm. He figured a few hours of innocent flirting, dinner, dancing and then bowling, and he'd have her agreeing to just about anything, but one look into the beauty's eyes had him craving for so much more.

Snap out of it.

Darnell gave a mental shake and realized Debra was talking to him.

"Dee, tell Jennifer I said happy birthday."

"I will." He strolled over, took the bag from her and reached for Liberty's before she could protest. "I'll carry it for you," he said and winked.

"Thanks." There was that sexy smile again. Oh, the things his mind was doing with those lips.

They waved goodbye and he pushed opened the door and the Christmas bell overhead tinkled. He stepped outside the door and waited until Liberty exited before he released it and fell into step beside her.

"It's snowing again!" she said with her head tilted allowing a snowflake to fall onto her tongue.

"I see," he said softly as he watched it slide across her tender pink lips. *Oh but he was in trouble.*

Reaching down, he laced his fingers with hers and dragged her closer. Side by side, hips brushing as they moved back up Main Street. Cars drove by and a few drivers blew their horns. He waved, not at all bothering to identify who was sitting behind the wheel as he focused on Liberty. Sheraton Beach towns were famous for gossip, and he knew he and Liberty were going to be a hot topic this week.

"I wanna talk to you about Christmas?"

Tilting her head, she looked up at him. "What about?"

"Santa… and presents," he said and realized he was actually excited about the upcoming holiday. "Does, Chance believe in Santa?"

He loved the way Liberty sucked in the air through her nose. "Yes, he believes in Santa Claus."

"Good, then I would like to be Santa this year."

"Really?" she said, eyes twinkling with amusement. "That's some big shoes to fill."

"Really?"

Liberty scrunched up her nose. "Uh-huh. I'm serious. A size nine to be exact," she said and stopped long enough to hold up her boot.

Darnell chuckled heartily, his deep voice roaring down the street. "I've been wearing a size thirteen since high school. I think I can handle it."

"We'll see," she teased.

"I love a challenge but since this is my first rodeo, how about we pick an afternoon and go shopping for my lil' man together?" he suggested.

She nodded. "Sounds like a plan."

On the drive to the gym, she rattled off a long list of things that Chance wanted for Christmas.

"It sounds like Chance needs to get a job!" he said with a chuckle and Liberty joined in. Once again the sound did crazy things to his insides.

He pulled up in front of the gym then jumped out and walked around and opened the door for her.

"Thank you so much for the cupcakes," she gestured with a sweep of the bags in her hand.

"Anytime."

Darnell knew he should stay far away from her but instead he studied her mouth, remembering the feel of those beautiful lips moving with skill and confidence against his.

"I'll see you tomorrow."

He was barely listening as he watched her slide her tongue nervously across her lips. "Oh yeah, right. I'll see you tomorrow."

While still staring at her lips, he reached for Liberty and gave her a chance to pull away. When she didn't, he dragged her closer, until her breasts were pillowed against his chest.

Her breathless panting whispered over his nose. "Dee, I really don't think this is a good idea," she whispered, tilting her chin to gaze up at him. "I think we're both confusing what is happening for something that it isn't."

"Maybe, maybe not," he said, his gaze sliding over her face and back to her lips. "Either way, I still plan on tasting you again."

"But—," she said taking a step away from him and leaned back against the door of the SUV.

"No buts," he whispered, lowering his head to hers.

As soon as his lips brushed hers, Darnell felt that amazing zing spiraling through him. He applied pressure and with a moan her mouth opened and he swept inside. Within seconds he was lost in the sensation, the feel, the taste. His arms moved around her and with Liberty pressed against him, Darnell could feel her heart pounding beneath her breasts and knew his own heart matched that wild rhythm.

She arched against him and he swept her up lifting her off her feet, desperate to feel even more of her. He wanted much more. Liberty naked lying beneath him, him positioned between her parted thighs as he slid into her warm heat, then pounding over and over until they were both completely spent and exhausted.

Abruptly, Darnell jerked back as if he'd been shocked by some overwhelming force. But even with the distance between them, his blood was pumping through his veins as hot and thick as lava.

"This is crazy," Liberty panted, then shook her head as if she didn't want to believe what was happening between them.

Hell, he knew exactly how she felt. He'd been feeling this way ever since he'd walked into her gym. "Doesn't seem to matter," he said as he took a step closer to her.

An uneasy chuckle ripped from her throat. "We can't do this." Holding out her arm, she held him back.

"Why not?" He probably should listen to her but at the moment he just didn't really care.

"Because…" Darnell could see she was searching her brain for a good reason and apparently came up empty. Still struggling for breath, she added. "Because we're going to regret it later." She swept past him, chin lifted, and head held high.

"Goodbye, Lib," he said and chuckled softly.

She stopped, looked over her shoulder at him and said pointedly, "Goodbye, Dee."

Chapter Ten

"Can I get another beer?"

The attractive barmaid looked at him with a friendly golden-brown smirk. "Another root beer coming right up."

Darnell chuckled. He had been coming to the establishment long enough that Mackenzie knew his drink of choice. Although sometimes staying sober wasn't as easy as it was other days. She popped the cap off the bottle, then plopped it down on the bar in front of him. "Thanks."

While sipping from the bottle, he glanced around. Spanky's Bar & Grill was locally owned and operated in Sheraton Beach. Slamming wings, drinks, good music, a jazzy upscale atmosphere, this was the place to be to meet-up, network, and unwind. After seeing Liberty he'd had a long afternoon in court, another bitter divorce with parents selfish and willing to split up their kids to keep the other from getting sole custody. The judge had postponed his ruling until next week. Darnell drew a long breath. It was reasons like that that gave marriage a sour taste.

Darnell looked toward the entrance in time to see his sister Sheyna sauntering up to the bar. Wearing a burgundy skirt and jacket over a charcoal ruffled blouse, she looked beautiful and fabulous as ever.

"Hey big brother!" she said then leaned in and brushed a kiss on his cheek. "Why am I meeting you here? I thought you were picking up Daddy and

Jennifer?"

He raked a hand across the tapered stubble along his cheek. "I thought so too, but once I got there, Dad said he and Jennifer were *celebrating*," he said with quotation marks, "and he'd meet us at eight instead of seven."

Sheyna started giggling. "You interrupted his groove."

He frowned. "What groove? He's old."

"Shame on you! You better not let Daddy hear you," she scolded and climbed on the stool beside him.

Darnell chuckled. He was pleased to see his father was happy. He just preferred not to think about what the two of them were doing.

Sheyna was chewing on bar nuts when she said, "Tell me about this woman you were seen kissing."

"*Are you serious?*" He groaned. The gossiping was the one thing he hated about living in Sheraton Beach. "There's nothing to tell."

"That's not what I heard. Carol over at the Fox Hole said the two of you were going at it so hard in the parking lot she was about to suggest that you go and get a room."

Darnell stared over the chocolate beauty and shook his head. By tomorrow he and Liberty would be engaged to be married. "It was just a kiss."

"Uh-huh." Sheyna signaled for the bartender then rested an elbow on the counter and leaned in. "Why were you kissing her?"

A growl burst past his lips. "Last I checked I was the big brother."

Up came her arms in a playful toss. "And you still are, but I want to know what your intentions are if you're kissing your son's mother." She smiled. "Wow! That's going to take some getting used to. I have a nephew!"

Darnell couldn't resist a grin. Every time he thought about having a miniature version of himself roaming around the town, he couldn't do anything but smile. If his son turned out to be anything like him and Scott, Chance Simmons was going to be a force to be reckoned with. He frowned. As soon as his paternity was confirmed he was going to have to do something about giving Chance his last name. He already knew that wasn't going to be an easy conversation.

Darnell waited until after Sheyna ordered a drink before he said, "We're taking blood tests tomorrow."

Sheyna blew out a slow breath. "Wow! Have you told Daddy about all this?"

"I was planning to tell him tonight." He shook his head. "I don't know how he's going to feel about me donating sperm."

Her amber eyes sparkled with astonishment. "I still can't believe you did something like that."

Neither could he. "At least I no longer have to wonder if there was a child running around. I'll know because he's now a part of my life."

"Listen to you... talking like a parent." She slapped his knee while grinning at him. "What's his mother like?"

He took a moment to think and then tried to keep the emotion out of his voice as he spoke. "Beautiful. Stubborn, very protective. She owns that new gym."

Her eyes widened, clearly impressed. "I heard their spinning classes are phenomenal."

He grinned. "So I've heard."

His sister studied him for a long moment before saying, "Are you thinking about having a relationship with Liberty?"

Darnell answered without hesitation. "No I'm just

trying to get to know my son's mother."

"Then what was all that kissing about?" Sheyna was watching him carefully, eyes narrowed.

"Are we back to that again?" Briefly, he squeezed his eyes shut.

"There's nothing wrong with having a relationship. I told you before at some point you'll have to stop hanging out at those strip clubs with Dax and Patrick," she said with an exaggerated eye roll.

He chuckled. "I'll have you know I haven't been at a strip club in weeks."

"I noticed you said weeks… not months. I guess that's a start." Mackenzie came back and set an amaretto sour on the bar in front of her.

"By the way, you better be bringing my new nephew to JJ's party."

He nodded. "Both of them are coming."

"*Both of them*?" He didn't miss the speculative look on his sister's face. "We're just friends, Shey-Shey."

"I think there's more going on than you want to admit." She grinned. "I can't wait to meet her."

♥ ♥ ♥

Dee, what are you doing?

Darnell hit the steering wheel with his fist. He had no idea and didn't have the time to care. All day… all evening, Liberty had been on his mind, and unless he did something about it there was no way he was getting any rest tonight.

Dinner with his family had been nothing short of enjoyable. During dessert he told his father about the sperm clinic and working to maintain a relationship with his son. And by the time dinner was over, and he was driving home, Darnell knew there was only one place he wanted to be tonight.

Picking up his phone, he typed in the code then scrolled through his call log and when he found the number he wanted, he hit Call. While he waited for the phone to be answered, he tapped his thumb impatiently against his thigh.

"Hello."

There was nothing sexier than a hint of sleep in her voice.

"Hey, it's me," he whispered as if he was trying not to disturb her sleep.

She yawned and purred, "Hey *It's Me*. What are you doing?"

"I'm parked outside your house."

There was a slight pause. "Why didn't you ring the doorbell?"

"Because I didn't want to wake Chance." It was his turn to pause. "Come down and open the door." Before she had a chance to object, he ended the call. Dragging in a long breath, he tried to clear his head and make sure he was thinking rationally. *There's no other way*, he told himself. The thing that had been brewing between them, he had to get it out his system once and for all.

Darnell took the key out of the ignition, opened the door, and climbed out of his Range Rover. By the time he climbed the steps, he heard a lock turn and then the door swung open. Liberty stood there in blue flannel pajamas.

"Hey sexy," he said with a smirk and stepped inside. Liberty closed the door and slowly turned around, staring up at him.

"What are you doing here?"

She was standing close and smelling wonderful. Her wild hair was pulled back in a ponytail at the top of her head. The two-piece pajamas were oversized and yet looked sexy as hell.

"I needed to see you," Darnell explained, as he shrugged out of his leather coat and draped it across the stair railing.

"Why?" she asked, eyes searching his.

He had never seen a more beautiful woman. He was way over his head, and yet he didn't care.

Before that nagging inner voice could change his mind, Darnell reached out, took Liberty's hand and pulled her against his chest. There was no point in wasting time. He knew why he was there and Liberty was about to find out.

"Dee..." she whispered.

"I love when you say my name," he told her and slowly lowered his mouth to hers, giving her the kiss he'd been yearning for all evening.

Liberty gave into the pressure of his mouth, meeting his strokes before placing a hand to his chest and turning away slightly. "I told you, I don't think this is a good idea," she protested.

"I think it's a perfect idea," Darnell said and tilted her chin so she had no choice but to look up at him. As soon as their eyes locked, he licked his lips and leaned toward her. "Now that we've come to an agreement, let's get to the reason for my visit."

Once again, he brought his mouth over hers, certain that what he had felt the last two times had been flukes, a trick of the mind, and this kiss wouldn't even come close in comparison, but it was far from the truth. Her plump lips were softer, her breath sweeter, and the sweep of her tongue was far more confident and arousing than before.

Yep. He was in trouble.

He teased her mouth with his tongue and slipped inside. His strokes became possessive with her matching him skillfully and ripping the air from his lungs. He was hard, rocking his hips, and grinding his erection against her. He tried to calm the rage that had settled into his mind but the more he kissed Liberty, the more out of control he became until he was suddenly overwhelmed with the need to be buried deep inside of her.

"I want you," he said in a strained voice. "So if you don't want me… tell me now."

He sucked her bottom lip into his mouth. Her nails dug into his chest as she whispered, "Yes, Dee, I want you."

With a sigh, his hand slipped beneath her top and eased up to palm her breast. Liberty was a perfect C-cup.

"Dee, not here," Liberty said between breaths. "Chance might see us."

Reluctantly, Darnell released her then took Liberty's hand and tugged her up the stairs where she pointed to the room on his left. He led her inside, shutting the door behind them.

♥ ♥ ♥

Liberty secured the lock on the door. Her heart was pounding. Hands were shaking. She had been imagining this moment and was starting to think that maybe she was still dreaming. And yet there Darnell was, sitting on the edge of her bed, waiting. What was it about this gorgeous man that she was so drawn to? She was starting to think, what's not to like? And, on the other hand, she just didn't care anymore. One night. That's all she needed was one night and after that she was certain she would get him out of her thoughts, and her dreams.

Or die trying.

"C'mere," he growled.

"Not yet," she replied softly. Her insides were shaking so hard it made her voice quiver.

Slowly, she unbuttoned her pajama top one at a time, starting from the bottom with her eyes never leaving his. To her delight desire glittered in his golden eyes. She had his full attention, making her feel like the most sexiest woman on earth, easing some of her nervousness. Darnell was seated, legs spread, his elbows resting on his knees. She swallowed when she saw his cock straining against his slacks. And then her gaze rose back to the wicked heat smoldering in the depth of his eyes.

She'd never seen a more beautiful man.

When she released the last button, she let the fabric fall open, nipples hard and standing at attention, and Darnell released a long hiss. "C'mere," he repeated but more impatient this time.

"How about you come over here?" she purred.

"You don't have to ask me twice." Darnell closed the gap between them and she didn't resist as he ran both hands along the sides of her breasts and then down inside the waistband of her pajama bottoms, cupping her ass.

"God, babe, you are beautiful." His voice came out breathless, laced with lust and need.

She drew in a deep shudder as Darnell dragged her against the length of his erection that flinched in response. "I can't wait to be inside you."

His words sent sharp tingles of need straight to her pussy.

And then he kissed her, aligning his insatiable lips perfectly to hers. His kisses were strong, demanding and downright delicious. She couldn't get enough and probably because his mouth promised so much. Fire and desire inflamed her with need, sending cream sliding down her inner thigh.

"Let's take these off," he urged.

Hooking his thumbs over the edge of her pajama bottoms, Darnell dragged them down her legs and she stepped out, kicking the flannel away.

Large, warm hands then skimmed up her thighs, passing the slopes of her ass where they rested on bare skin heating with desire.

"Now it's your turn," Liberty purred, then tugged the hem of his shirt free, working at the buttons of his crisp white shirt until she could slide her fingers along the muscles rippling across his chest where she felt the rapid beat of his heart. Then she eased the shirt off his shoulders. *Oh my, he's sexy*, she thought, then realized she still had too many clothes on and slowly peeled away her own top. Naked, she stared up at Darnell, and drew in a deep breath.

"You're more beautiful than I imagined," he whispered while his warm hands slid over her bare skin, and around to her breasts.

"Thank you," she said leaning into his touch, savoring the way he felt caressing her.

Darnell cupped one hand between her thighs, then slid a finger through her folds. A gasp slipped from her throat. "You're wet," he growled, nostrils flaring. "You want this dick, don't you?"

With his thumb fondling her clit, she expelled a long shaky breath. The question was complicated and yet the simplest thing he could have ever asked. "Yes, I would like that," she confessed as pleasure snaked through her body.

"Then it's time to go to bed."

Taking her hand, Darnell led her over to the king-sized bed, and lowered onto the mattress with her straddling his thighs. He then cupped her head, drawing her toward his, and kissed her lips and neck. Reaching up, he removed the band from her hair so that it was curly, loose and free.

Laughing, she drew back. "Why'd you do that? My hair's a mess."

He shook his head and smiled. "No sweetheart. I love it this way."

His words caused her heart to turn over in her chest. He was amazing. His touch and the way he looked at her, gave her more pleasure than she'd ever known.

He took a nipple into his mouth and she cried out. "You like that?"

Like it? She loved his power and strength. Her pussy was wet and aching for his touch. She moaned as he captured the other between his fingers, his thumb traced her areola sending jolts of pleasure through her. While he suckled and teased her aroused nipples, she allowed her fingernails to graze up and down the contours of his arms, feeling the muscles contract. He bit down causing her to release a wild cry.

Chuckling, Darnell rolled her over onto her back. His large, warm hands skimmed every curve and then there was his lips and tongue, teasing and caressing, unleashing a firestorm that caused her nipples to harden like steel.

Liberty released his belt buckle then found his zipper and slid it down over his straining erection. She ran her fingers along his amazing length before peeling his pants down over his hips. She wanted and needed him now hard and deep inside her.

"Please tell me you brought a condom?" she asked and was practically begging. Liberty wasn't sure what she would do if he hadn't.

"I got you," he whispered, kissed her once more then rose from the bed, and removed a foil packet from his wallet. Her heart pounded violently as she watched Darnell step out of his pants. Her body quivered as he peeled his briefs away. He stood before her, muscles rippling across his abdomen. When his cock sprang into view, she wet her lips. It jutted upward, straining and swollen as he rolled on the condom..

That man is blessed.

Leaning over, he lifted Liberty into his arms, and shifted her up onto the bed until her head was on the pillow. Darnell dropped soft kisses across her skin as he crawled between her legs. Her body bucked and withered as his tongue took its sweet time until there wasn't a place on her that hadn't felt his lips.

"Lib, look at me," he commanded and brought her legs up around his waist. When she stared up into his powerful eyes, he grasped his cock and guided it to her waiting pussy. "You ready?"

She swallowed and nodded.

"Hold on," he murmured, then drove hard inside with one deep thrust.

She bit back a sharp cry. Darnell felt so good Liberty shuddered, and her eyelids closed as he stretched and filled her again. He hissed with male satisfaction that sent goose bumps down her spine.

"Open your eyes," he demanded.

She stared at him, gazes locked as he pumped between her thighs. Lust and desire darkened his eyes to a golden hue.

"I want you to see what I'm doing to you," Darnell murmured and drove deeper. She wrapped her legs around his hips, holding tight.

"Yes, yes," she panted as she dug her fingers into his shoulders. His hands gripped her hips, dragging her closer as they built a rhythm of their own. Every muscle in his body tightened and she struggled to hold on. He felt so good she wanted it to last as long as possible.

Darnell thrust harder. "Tell me who's fucking you, Lib?"

She gasped. "Dee… You're fucking me."

"And how does it feel?" he growled then gripped her hips pumping into her with greater force.

"Oh…, you… feel … sooo good!" she whimpered. "*Sooo* good…. Please don't stop."

"I wouldn't dream on it." he hissed. "Now come for me, Lib,"

Desperate need filled her body as Darnell pounded his hips at a frantic pace, the sensation powerful and overwhelming.

"Dee!" she wailed and then exploded around his cock. She bucked beneath him. Darnell groaned and thrust long, hard and deep before his body bucked and drove home with his release. Liberty sagged against the cover and exhaled.

Completely spent, Darnell rolled over onto his side. Snaking an arm around Liberty's waist, he brought her close to him and they clung to each other. The silence of the night stole over her as her heartbeat slowed and her breathing eased.

When Darnell had told her being here was a perfect idea, she had no idea just how right he had been. Sex with Darnell had been everything she could have imagined and nothing like anything she had ever experienced. It was supposed to be just one night and yet while lying in his arms, Liberty couldn't dream of being anywhere else but with him.

Now what? that inner voice taunted.

Liberty had no idea. She knew what she wanted,

but she also knew what he wanted as well. *Darnell Simmons doesn't do relationships.*

Liberty dozed off and woke hours later with her head resting on his chest, his arm draped over her waist, her legs entwined with his.

It hadn't been a dream.

Slowly, she eased out from under him. Darnell hadn't even stirred. As she stared down at him a smile turned the corner of her lips. *He definitely put his work in.*

Liberty slipped back into her pajamas and padded over to stare out the wide window. The snow had stopped. Outside was a white blanket of snow. Her body was still tingling from the power of Darnell's strokes and passion of their lovemaking. And she wanted more, so much more, only nothing good could come of that but heartache.

How was her life supposed to go back to normal after that?

Liberty wrapped her arms around her middle and continued to stare out into the dark of the night as images of their lovemaking replayed. Sex had never been that good. Even with Greg it had never been so passionate. And then the few encounters after him hadn't even come close to arousing her desire to have more. But with Darnell, making love had her thinking about things she had no idea even allowing to surface in her mind. What they'd had was a moment. And now that moment was over.

"You're up early."

She twirled around to see Darnell sitting up on the bed, and her traitorous eyes traveled hungrily up and down his amazing chest. The blanket was draped across the rest of him and for that she released a sigh of relief. "I've always been a light sleeper," she lied.

Grinning, he patted the spot beside him. "Then come back to bed."

Her nipples hardened. One more round was so tempting, but she also knew it would make the situation even more difficult to walk away from. "I think you probably need to go before Chance wakes up. I don't want to confuse him."

He stared at her as if he was ready to say something before he finally nodded. "Yeah, you're right. I'm sure things are going to become confusing enough for him as it is."

She forced a smile, touched that he understood, but a part of her was also disappointed he didn't insist on staying.

What did you think would happen?

Liberty watched as Darnell slipped out from the bed. Lust stormed her body at the sight of his long, thick cock swinging from a nest of dark pubic hair. She moaned low in her throat and licked her lips, resisting the urge to walk across the room and touch it.

Once his pants were on, he reached into his pocket for his keys and pointed a remote starter toward the window. "Might as well warm it up," he explained.

Nodding Liberty tore her eyes away from his amazing chest. She walked over to the closet and retrieved her robe. She slipped it on and tied the belt; the entire time she avoided eye contact. "I'll be in the living room," she said and brushed past him and went down the stairs away from the temptations of her bed. And a half-dressed Darnell Simmons.

She was curled up on the couch pretending to watch the eleven o'clock news when she heard him coming down the stairs. And then there he was, standing in the doorway.

"Oh, that was quick," she murmured and rose from

the couch and walked out into the foyer.

Darnell slipped on his jacket and moved towards her. Her heart sank. Already she could see the regret brimming in his eyes. "Listen, Lib, I'm sorry. I had no business—"

She raised her fingers to his lips and shook her head. "No need to explain. We both knew it was going to happen eventually." Eyes locked, Darnell took her hand in his. At the contact, Liberty released a shaky breath and said, "Now that we've gotten that out the way, we can get back to focusing on Chance."

His eyes searched her speculatively before he pulled her to him and lowered his mouth to hers. Liberty brought her arms around his waist and moaned as his tongue slipped inside, stroking hers. "Thank you for tonight," he rasped against her mouth.

She choked out a laugh and then pushed away. "You're welcome. Now get out of here before it starts snowing again."

Darnell flashed a quick, sexy smile before he headed out the door without uttering another word.

It was better that way.

Chapter Eleven

He looked up from his desk at his assistant. "Brenda, see if you can get the dictation on the Galicia's case done before you leave. I would like to have the petition filed at the courthouse first thing in the morning. Also, ask Mrs. Austin to come in tomorrow and sign the separation agreement."

She nodded. "Will there be anything else Mr. Dee?"

She was an attractive Asian woman, petite, in her early thirties, with long dark hair and slanted brown eyes. When she had first started working for them five years ago, she had no idea how she was going to refer to her three bosses when all of their last names were Simmons. They decided they would be the only attorneys at the law firm she would call by their nicknames.

"No, that will be all."

Nodding, she lifted a binder from his desk and carried it over to a bookshelf on the wall. She then walked over to a small conference table and retrieved several client files that needed to be put away and cupped the folders to her chest. The mother of three never could resist tidying up his space. "Have a good evening," she finally said.

He smiled. "Thanks Brenda, and the same to you."

As soon as she left, he went through his mail then reached down for his phone and looked down at the screen. *Damn. Nothing*! After lunch he had sent Liberty a text message.

Thinking of you.

And he had yet to hear back from her.

What the hell was wrong with him?

There was a light knock and he looked up to see Patrick strolling into his office swinging the leather briefcase his mother had given him as a graduation gift after he'd passed the bar.

"Hey Pat. Was that a new client?" Darnell said leaning back on the chair with his hands laced behind his head.

Patrick scowled as he walked across the carpet toward his large oak desk. "Yep. Another couple battling over money." He took the seat across from his desk and shared the details of his newest divorce case.

They went back and forth until Darnell lost his train of thought and found himself thinking about the other night.

He was used to one-night stands, but nothing had ever come close to what he had felt the other night. Liberty had managed to turn his world upside down. And that wasn't easy to do. In fact, he rarely if ever thought about a woman after the fact, even if she had been a beast in bed. It was all about the conquest, but with Liberty even after sex, Darnell couldn't seem to get her off his mind. He'd been torturing himself time and time again by rewinding their lovemaking; the memories so vivid, each flashback left him thick and hard. What was even worse was the thoughts were so often he was having a hard time thinking about anything else.

He had even started going to *24/7 Fitness* at lunch just so he'd have an excuse to stop by Liberty's office, but each time she rushed off claiming she had errands to run.

It was crazy. Clearly insane that he was so consumed with one woman. He wasn't interested in a relationship and definitely not with his son's mother. That would just complicate things. He was trying to build a relationship with his son, and he didn't need anything standing in the way of that. Especially not Liberty. Although he had a sinking feeling she was avoiding him. His inner voice kept reminding him it was better this way. That they'd both gotten what they wanted. That it was now time for him to move on.

"Yo, Dee. You listening?"

He blinked rapidly, then cleared his throat. "Sure. I'm listening."

Patrick gave him a weird look. "Nah, I could tell your mind was somewhere other than here. What's been up with you lately? You haven't been yourself."

"What are you talking about?" Darnell asked, while shifting uncomfortably on his executive chair.

He straightened his tie, clearly looking amused. "What I'm talking about is that you've been off your game. You're usually the first one here and the last one to leave, expecting everyone else to do the same, but now you're not here even when you are here."

Darnell simply shrugged. "Now that I've have Chance, he's the priority."

"Are you sure that's all it is?" Patrick leaned back on the chair, eyeing him speculatively. "Rumor around town is you've been spending a lot of time with that pretty new aerobics instructor."

He dragged a hand down his face. Why was he even surprised? "Nope," he replied, carefully. "We're just trying to work together for our son."

"I saw the two of you at Upscale." Patrick chuckled, wagging his head at him. "Keep thinking that man."

"What?"

With a roll of his eyes, his cousin rose to his feet. "First Scott... now you. What's this world turning into?"

"I haven't changed," Darnell denied.

Patrick's lips twitched as he stared down at him. "Yes you have. You're just too stubborn to admit it."

Darnell merely laughed then waited until Patrick departed his office before he sprung from the chair and released a deep breath. He was too restless to just sit. Patrick was wrong. He wasn't looking for a relationship, and neither was Liberty. He had gotten what he had set out for. To win over Liberty, show her how great a guy he was so that he could be a part of his son's life. And that's all he had been after. Nothing more. His life was fine just the way it was.

Now he had to find a way to get his mind and body to understand that.

♥ ♥ ♥

The next week they settled into a routine. Liberty taught her aerobic classes at night and Darnell picked Chance up from daycare and hung out together until she got off. Once she left the gym, she would swing by his place where Chance was bathed and ready for bed in his footie pajamas beneath his winter coat. By doing so she avoided any alone time with him, which was for the best. Although the attraction was always there simmering and sparking.

It was maddening. Darnell was Chance's father. The blood test was a ninety-nine-point-nine-nine match, not that she was at all surprised. The more times she saw the two of them together, there was no denying how much they not only resembled, but had in common.

She didn't want to like him. It was supposed to just be about Chance and Darnell and their relationship, only he was getting to her. Somehow he had managed to wiggle his way into her thoughts. Her traitorous body definitely remembered who he was and tightened every time she recalled that smile or his swag. And any time he was near, her entire body heated and her nipples hardened and ached for his long strong fingers to touch them.

But it wasn't just the physical attraction. Over the last week they'd talked and laughed. One afternoon Darnell had even called her from his office to tell her about plans he had for Chance during the holidays and they ended up laughing for almost thirty minutes about some hair-brain stunt he and his brother had done one holiday season. And then there were the days he dropped by the gym to work out and when she saw the muscle t-shirt straining across his chest, her entire body was flaming so hot, she had to get out the building as quick as possible, otherwise she would have demanded he fuck her on top of her desk. *It was crazy!* Darnell consumed her thoughts and her body, and she decided the best thing to do was to stay away from him, regardless of how exhausting fighting her attraction had started to become.

Liberty was slipping into her coat when she heard her cell phone ring. She fumbled through her purse and brought the phone to her ear. It was Darnell.

"Hey, my lil' man is knocked out. How about he stay over here tonight?"

Her heart pounded at the husky sound in her ear. "Uh no, that's okay. He has a routine and I really don't want to change that just yet." It was hard enough getting Chance to settle down after spending the evening with Darnell. It was Mr. Dee this, and Mr. Dee that, and if he stayed over she would never be able to get him to go to daycare in the morning. "I'm on my way now," she told him as she flicked off her light.

"Okay." She ignored the disappointment in his voice and ended the call.

Not long after, Liberty pulled into the driveway and killed the engine. She gazed out the window, admiring Darnell's oversized colonial with magnificent ocean views. Self-consciously, she smoothed a hand across her hair, then pulled the hood down over her head and climbed out the SUV. The air was cold and biting at her cheeks as she hurried toward the porch, and she had barely raised her hand to knock on the door when it flung open.

"Get in here," Darnell said, grinning warmly as he stepped aside.

"Thanks," she murmured and hurried into the comfort of his home.

He shut out the wind then turned around, rubbing his hands together. "It's cold tonight."

"Yes it is," she agreed. Liberty stared up at him and noticed a shadow had grown on his square jaw, accentuating everything male about him. "I better get going while my vehicle is still warm."

"Why the rush?" he asked and signaled with a wave of his hand for her to follow him to the rear of the house.

Liberty released a long shaky breath debating if she should insist or not and in the end, she wiped her feet on the rug at the front of the door and followed him. She walked down the long hall covered in dark wood flooring through a large dream eat-in kitchen with stainless steel appliances, Quartz countertops, and a large island. On the other side was a family room with floor-to-ceiling windows on the wall facing the ocean.

Soft jazz music was playing from a stereo system on a huge wall unit and a fire was crackling at the center of the room. Panic kicked in. The scene was nothing short of romantic.

"I really should be going," she insisted.

Darnell was standing near the fireplace when he turned and looked at her. "Lib, Why the rush? I thought maybe we could sit and roast some marshmallows."

When she spotted the bag in his hands, she started laughing. "Marshmallows? There's no way I can pass that up. I'll stay for a little while." She shrugged out of her coat and draped it over the end of a large black-leather sectional that dominated the space.

"Take your boots off," he insisted.

She only hesitated briefly before pulling off her UGGs and then padded across the plush carpeting over to the fireplace and took a seat on the floor beside him, Indian-style. "Okay, hand me one," she said holding out her hand.

Laughing, Darnell gave her a stick. "Now, roasting marshmallows takes skills."

"Oh it does, does it?" she teased as she poked two through the middle.

He looked over, eyes twinkling with mischief.

"What?" she asked.

"I have another surprise," he whispered.

"What?" she asked with a smile.

She watched as Darnell reached underneath a pillow and then held up a package.

Her eyes widened as she burst out with laughter. "Hershey bars?"

Every time he gave her that boyish grin, he reminded her so much of Chance. "I thought we could make some s'mores."

Her eyes crinkled with laughter. "I haven't made these since I was a kid."

"Well then you're in for a treat. My lil' man and I made some this evening. He ended up with chocolate and marshmallows all over his clothes."

"I can just imagine." She grinned and pushed a piece of chocolate between two marshmallows then lifted the stick in front of the fire.

"We had such a good time I think I wore him out."

While they made s'mores, Darnell gave her a recap of their evening which started with a snowball fight and ended with a bubble bath. While he talked, she saw the pride in his eyes. She stared at him smiling. In such a short time, Darnell had made an impression on her son. Every time she saw them together she felt this overwhelming emotion she couldn't explain. One thing for sure—she was glad Chance finally had a father.

They sat there enjoying each other's company until the last marshmallow was roasted and her legs began to cramp. "Oh, I'm getting old," she groaned.

Darnell offered her a hand and lifted her into a standing position. "Not you. You work out every day."

She smiled. "Yeah, but that doesn't mean I'm not getting any older." Liberty wasn't sure how long she stood there, staring up at him. No words were being said. They didn't need it. The soft music filled the silence of the room and continued to send a romantic vibe to the space.

Darnell reached up and caressed the side of her face with his hand as he said, "I like being around you, Lib."

She was thinking the same thing. She enjoyed being around him, talking and laughing. "So do I."

His hand dropped to her shoulder, and her breasts tingled and tightened as his fingers slid down along her arm until he reached her hand and laced her fingers with his. "Have you seen *The Best Man Holiday*?"

"With Morris Chestnut?" She swallowed then shook her head. "No I haven't."

Desire blazed in his eyes as he tugged at her hand, drawing her closer. "Then stay and watch it with me."

It was after nine and she knew she should get as far away from him as possible. For the last week she had been doing everything she could to avoid him. Leaving her SUV running while she dashed in to get Chance, yet today she hadn't. Why? she wondered.

You know why!

She knew that whatever time they had, it would be all she would get, and she might as well enjoy it while it lasted. She was certain eventually Darnell would get bored and move on to his next conquest, and she was prepared for it. But right now being around him gave her a chance to get to know him better and find out for sure his being in Chance's life wasn't just a phase... that he was as committed to being a father as he was to his law practice... she was using him as much as he was possibly using her. And as long as she kept repeating it she just might start believing everything happening between them was about Chance, not them.

With that in mind, she allowed Darnell to lead her over to the couch where she sank back into the cushions, determined to enjoy every second of their time together. She was sure after the holidays, it would be over and then all she would have were the memories.

They watched the movie, and the entire time she was physically aware of him sitting beside her. Their feet were up on an ottoman, legs intertwined while they munched away at microwave popcorn. And by the time the closing credits rolled neither of them made any move to stand. Liberty continued to sit there, listening to her heart beat.

"Don't go. Not yet," Darnell said as though he knew if she got up from the couch it would be time for her to leave.

With a remote, he clicked off the television and turned back on the jazz. They sat there facing one another, his hand resting on her thigh.

"What do you want for Christmas?" he asked.

"What?" she gasped.

"You heard me. I want to know what you want for Christmas." He reached for her hand and interlocked his fingers with hers.

"I don't know," she said with a shrug. "What do you want for Christmas?"

He looked at her, his eyes with emotions she couldn't even begin to explain dancing in their depths. "You've already given me the best gift. My son."

His words warmed her in so many ways.

"Well in that case I already have my Christmas present as well. You have given my son so much joy. That means more to me than any gift you could buy." Her eyes glossed over with unshed tears. Liberty frowned.

Darnell wiped the corners of her eyes with the pad of his thumb. "Don't get all emotional on me now," he teased.

She laughed. "I can be a crybaby at times."

He chuckled along with her.

When she sobered, she dragged a leg up to her chest and said, "I do want to talk to you about something."

"What is it?" he asked lightly.

She sat back and stared at him for a long moment

before saying, "When do you want to tell Chance you're his father?"

"If it was up to me I'd be waking up my lil' man and telling him now," he laughed then paused and searched her eyes. "But I think that's something you need to decide."

Liberty took a deep breath. Part of her believed he was too young to even really understand, but the other part knew Chance would be happy to finally have someone to call Daddy. "Maybe after the holidays we can tell him together."

His grin widened. "I like that idea." Darnell pulled her close and she lowered her head on his shoulder.

"You regret what we did the other night, don't you?" he asked.

Raising her head, she stared up at him. "How could I possibly regret that?"

He studied her, his eyes probing her. "Because ever since, you've been avoiding me."

"No I —."

"Lib, you have," he interrupted, then lifted her up and over until she was sitting across his lap.

She sighed. "Okay, maybe I have. I just figured it was best not for that to happen again." Liberty shrugged and wet her lips nervously. "I like what we have and I don't want to ruin that."

His hand slid across her back, sending a shiver down her spine. "I don't want to ruin it either. You're a special woman. Chance is one lucky little boy."

"Thank you." Lovingly, he pressed his lips to her forehead.

Goodness, this man was making things difficult for her. Even though they had an understanding and wouldn't do anything to jeopardize their relationship with Chance, he unknowingly had set a standard.

Darnell had so far outshone any other man she'd ever dated that it was impossible to imagine ever meeting another man who could even come close.

Oh God! She was in serious trouble.

They lay on the couch talking about everything and nothing. She'd never shared so much of her past with anyone and felt honored by the trust he showed in sharing his past with her.

"Lib, I'm attracted to you. There's no denying that. I just have so many emotions swimming around in my head with finding out about Chance that I don't want to confuse that and make you think there's more going on than it is."

She swallowed a lump of despair. "I totally understand." He didn't want her falling in love and getting all clingy. *Got it.*

"I like you and I don't want to jeopardize that."

"I agree. You're not looking for a relationship. Well, neither am I," she said. His lips were so close. Liberty wanted to kiss him. She wanted to kiss him bad.

Darnell brought his hand up and rubbed a thumb up and down her jaw. "But that doesn't mean I don't want to hold and kiss you every chance I can." His face took on a totally different intensity when he locked his fierce amber gaze with hers.

"Is that so?" Her voice hitched when he brought his lips to the side of her neck.

"Absolutely. I'm attracted to you Lib," he said. "Your hair, your body. Hell I get a hard on just from hearing your voice on the phone."

His hand slid down to her stomach and began toying with the seam of her bra. Liberty knew she should push his hands away, but instead she reached around behind her back and unclasped the hooks.

Darnell growled in approval. "Did you ever come while you were talking on the phone with me?"

How did he know?

She moaned when his hand slid under one of the cups of her bra.

"Did you?" he asked palming her breasts possessively.

"Yes," she groaned.

"I love your breasts," he growled and Liberty arched off his lap when his fingers pinched her nipple. "Do you like when I play with your titties?"

"Oh yes," she breathed. "That's my spot."

"Right here?" he asked as he tweaked her nipple between his thumb and forefinger.

"Yesss," she exhaled. "Right there."

He brought his other hand up, assaulting both her nipples at once, using the pad of his thumbnails, then looked at Liberty to gauge her reaction. She moaned and arched her body toward him.

"I love the way your breath speeds and slows every time I touch you here. Are you wet?"

His words caused desire to bloom in her stomach. She moaned and squeezed her thighs together. Darnell had the ability to make her cream in her panties with mere erotic words. The combination of his hands and voice was enough to make her come on herself.

Reaching down, he unfastened the top button of her jeans and then slowly lowered her zipper. "Lift up," he urged and she wasted no time raising her hips just enough so he could ease her jeans slightly down. As soon as he had better access, he slipped his fingers past the crotch of her panties and eased between the soft folds of her pussy.

"Sweetheart, I have to touch you." His words came out breathless.

"God, I've never wanted something so bad," she groaned.

"Neither have I."

Darnell gently penetrated her with two fingers, sliding in and out, and her body shivered with desire. Liberty tried to spread her legs as far as she could with her jeans in the way.

"I was right. You are wet," he hissed. "Damn." He removed his fingers and brought them to his mouth and sucked. "Baby, you taste good."

Her breath caught in her throat. She couldn't even find the words to speak, and the next time when he pushed inside her pussy, she rocked her hips and met him halfway. "Mmmm, oh yeah," she moaned as Darnell pumped his fingers, sliding them between the soft folds then stroked his thumb over her clit. His other hand was caressing her breasts and driving her crazy. Liberty lifted her hips, rocking into the strokes of his fingers, loving the feeling of him sliding around in her cream. Soon, she was moaning and panting. She was so close. She wanted... She needed...

The doorbell rang.

They both startled.

Her eyes snapped to his. "Who is that?"

"I'm not sure but, whoever it is I hope they left the motor running." He removed his hand from her panties, and Liberty cried out in protest.

"Sorry babe," Darnell whispered. With a frustrated sigh, she slipped off his lap onto the cushion beside him

While Liberty zipped her jeans, she watched as Darnell rose and walked out the room. She wasn't sure who was at his door. However, the interruption was definitely the jolt of reality she needed.

♥ ♥ ♥

Darnell scowled as he hurried to the front of the house. Talk about bad timing. He was horny. With every step he felt his hard dick straining against his zipper. Damn. In a few more minutes he would have had those pretty legs wrapped around his face.

There's nothing he could do about it now.

Taking a ragged breath, he dragged a hand down his face and then opened the door. A beautiful woman stood on his steps.

He gaped at her incredulously... "Karine?"

"Hey Dee, I thought I would drop by with this pie." She sauntered past him and stood in the foyer, wearing a long black wool coat and high heel suede boots.

And Darnell bet good money there was nothing on underneath.

"Here, this is for you." She held out her pie that even had a nice red bow.

He took it from her proffered hands. "How did you find out where I lived?"

She gave a coy smile. "It wasn't that hard. I just let my fingers do the walking." Smiling, her eyes swept the twelve-foot ceiling. "Very nice."

"Karine, this is really a bad time."

She pouted. "That's too bad. I wanted to give you your Christmas present." Before he could stop her, she unfastened the belt and her coat swung open.

Darnell swallowed. Yep, he had been right. She was wearing nothing but lacy red panties and red bows covered each nipple.

Frantically he looked toward the family room.

"Listen you have to leave. I have company."

"*Company?*" she snapped. "Who?"

"Mr. Dee, I'm thirsty."

His head jerked toward the top of the stairs where Chance was standing. "Sure Lil' Man. I'll be right up with something for you to drink."

Karine snatched her coat closed. "Who is that?"

"My son. The question is, who are you?"

Karine swung around to see where that voice had come from. Darnell's brow rose as he spotted Liberty coming down the hall with that fire back in her eyes. He swore long and hard. This couldn't be happening.

"Lib, I got this," he said and stared at her, waiting for Liberty to look at him so she could see he had no idea she was coming over, but Liberty avoided eye contact.

"Who is that?" Karine snarled, swinging around with attitude.

Liberty was about to tell her when he blocked her path and replied, "Karine, she's none of your business. Now I would like for you to leave." Gently he swung his unwanted guest around and led her over to the door.

"But I just got here," she whined.

"And now it's time to go." Darnell fought to control his anger.

"Call me later so we can finish where we left off," she said with a wink, then stepped through the door.

Darnell blew out a frustrated breath and waited until Karine was safely in her car before he shut the front door with a click. By the time he found them in the living room, Liberty was helping Chance into his coat.

"You don't have to leave."

She didn't even bother to look his way. "Yes we do. I need to get Chance to bed."

"Mr. Dee, see you later," he said in a sleepy voice.

She zipped his coat and he started toward the door. Avoiding eye contact, Liberty tried to walk past him, but he reached for her arm, and stopped her.

"I don't want you to leave," he declared, flashing his grin.

Liberty hiked her chin stubbornly and said, "Really, and why is that?"

His eyes bored into hers. "You know why."

"And is that the only reason?" she asked and, after a long moment of silence, she shook her head. "I can't do this Darnell. You *don't* want a relationship. You *don't* want me to leave. What do you want, Dee?" With exasperation she tossed her hands in the air. "We need to quit because someone's going to get hurt."

Guiltily, Darnell didn't stop her this time. Instead he grabbed his coat and shoes near the door, walked out and made sure Chance was strapped safely in his car seat before he stepped back and watched her drive away.

Liberty was right. It wasn't fair. Until he knew what he wanted the smartest thing was to stay away. He just wasn't sure if he could do that.

Chapter Twelve

"Ooh Mommy, look!"

Liberty followed the direction of his finger and her eyes widened. "Wow! You see that?"

"Yaay!" Chance was squealing in the backseat.

They were traveling up a long windy road with trees covered in decorative holiday lights. Further up the road she saw a grand farmhouse. Lights were twinkling and in the large front window was a huge Christmas tree.

"What a beautiful house!"

Darnell took his eyes briefly off the road and said, "It was Jace's gift to my sister when he proposed and they've been adding wings to it ever since."

She nodded. "I can see why. It's lovely."

Cars were parked all along the large circular driveway. Her pulse raced at the thought of meeting not only Darnell's family, but some of the Beaumonts as well. She was excited for Chance who was finally going to meet his relatives.

After the incident at Darnell's house, she had considered not coming, but Chance had insisted. She was a little worried. Would Chance understand that she wasn't always going to share the life he now had with Darnell? She spent most of the night pondering the possible dilemma, and decided after the holidays she would start allowing Darnell to start keeping Chance overnight so their son could get used to just the two of them doing things together. But for now, she was just going to find out what it was like to share the holidays with family.

Darnell had barely put the SUV in Park when Chance was climbing out his car seat. "Hold tight Lil' Man and let me get you out," Darnell said with a chuckle.

Liberty looked over her shoulder and grinned at Chance. His eyes were wide with excitement. Warmth flooded her heart. He was happy. Darnell made him happy. That was clear to see. While he helped Chance from the back, Liberty blinked away tears and removed her own seatbelt. *They'll be none of that today,* she warned. Not waiting for Darnell to come around, she opened the door, stepped out and the heel of her boot slipped on ice and she cried out. Before she hit the ground, Darnell raced around the Range Rover and caught her. Liberty found her chest pressed up against his.

"You gotta be careful," he murmured and she gazed up into his beautiful eyes and for a moment she forgot where she was.

"Thank you."

He smirked and leaned forward until their lips were almost touching.

"Come on Mommy!" Chance called breaking the spell. He was tossing snow in the air.

"I guess we better get inside," Darnell said. Liberty nodded and took a step back. "Here, hold my hand. I don't need you falling and tryna sue my family, then I would have to represent you."

She gave him a teasing smile. "Since when did you become an accident lawyer?"

He winked. "I would make an exception for you."

Goodness. What was this man trying to do, make

her fall in love? Liberty pushed that thought aside. Today was all about her son.

She put her gloved hand in his and followed his lead up the paved sidewalk, admiring the large plastic candy canes that lined both sides of the lawn. As they drew closer, she heard festive music and laughter coming from inside.

Once they were on the porch, Darnell pushed open one of the large mahogany hurricane doors, and they followed him inside to a lavish foyer that boasted a crystal chandelier and gleaming wood flooring. "Hey Hey Hey…, we're here!" he announced as they stepped into a great room with high ceilings and exposed cherry beams. There were collective *oohs* and *aahs* and immediately the guests started greeting them all at once. The women rushed to fuss over Chance, while Liberty's hand was shook by one person after another. The first face she recognized was Darnell's father.

"Young lady, it's a pleasure to see you again," Mr. Simmons said with a wide grin, then he dragged Liberty into a warm hug.

"Thank you all for inviting us," she replied once he released her.

"Of course, you're now family."

Family. If only that were true.

He pointed to his right. "You remember my wife?"

Liberty looked over at the short woman she had met in the grocery store. Jennifer was pretty with dark-brown hair that she wore tapered close showing off her diamond-studs. Tonight she was dressed conservatively in dark slacks and a red turtleneck sweater. Jennifer had to be years younger, but it was apparent with these two, age didn't matter. "Yes, of course. It's good to see you again."

She hurried over and gave Liberty a big squeeze

then pulled back with a warm, curious look twinkling in her light gray eyes. "Where's that little boy of yours?"

Liberty whipped around and found Chance was no longer standing in the doorway, although his coat, he had dropped onto the floor. She reached down and retrieved it.

"I think the kids have already grabbed him," Jennifer said and Liberty followed the direction of her finger to the other side of the large room where the adults were mingling and the kids were in the corner playing with toys.

"Which one's the birthday boy?" Liberty asked. She was still holding his gift in her hand. Jennifer pointed to an adorable dark-skinned boy, who was laughing and playing with Chance.

"That's Jace Jr. over there."

"Here, I'll take your gift and put it with the rest," Mr. Simmons offered. Before he took the large, blue gift bag, he squeezed her hand. "Thank you so much. You made an old man quite happy." His amber eyes were misty and Liberty felt herself blinking away tears of her own.

"Thank you for opening up your heart to my son."

He shrugged a beefy shoulder. "He's a Simmons and family means everything to us."

Jennifer held out her hand. "Let me take those coats from you."

Liberty slipped out of her long wool coat, handed over Chance's, then glanced down at the red sweater dress and found it twisted. She was adjusting it when Darnell came strutting over.

"Come, let me introduce you to the crew." Darnell took her hand and led her across the Brazilian cherry flooring toward a grand piano. "Lib, this is my sister

Sheyna and that's her husband Jace behind the bar, screwing up drinks." His comment caused the group to roar with laughter.

Jace was quick with a punch. "Very funny. You never seemed to have a problem with those Tom Collins I used to make you."

Darnell rubbed his chin. "Hmmm that might be why I stopped drinking."

There was more laughter when Sheyna sashayed over and wrapped an arm around her shoulders. "Welcome to my home. My nephew is adorable."

"Thank you." Liberty was so overwhelmed she didn't know what else to say." She was in the same house with the Beaumonts! She gazed at the mahogany beauty. She could see the family resemblance. Sheyna's eyes were golden like Darnell's but slanted, almost exotic. She wore her hair in bouncy shoulder-length curls, and she was so petite Liberty was certain the woman ate like a bird.

"I hear you're the owner of that hot new gym," Sheyna inquired.

Another woman rushed over. "You own *that* gym? Hi, I'm Bianca, Jace's sister. I've been planning to join," she said, walnut-colored eyes sparkling with interest.

Smiling, Liberty shook her hand. "Please do, I offer a one-week free membership just to come and try it out."

"Can I come too?" chimed in another attractive woman as she sauntered her voluptuous curves over to the two and held out her hand. "Hi, I'm Zanaa. I'm married to Dee's brother." She gave a playful eye roll but there was no missing the admiration in her gaze.

"Scott, right?" Liberty asked as she tried to keep the names straight.

Zanaa nodded and pushed a lock of brown hair

away from her face. "Yes, that's him standing off to the right, being the center of attention as usual." Liberty scanned the area until she found the one who closely resembled Darnell. Same height and build, Scott's eyes were dark, his skin the color of almonds and then there were definitely a few other differences. Liberty shivered just thinking about Darnell's delicious mouth in particular.

Sheyna gave a rude snort. "My brother has always been a clown."

She smiled and searched the room for Darnell and found him sitting on the couch talking to his father. Lazily, she admired his beard that had been trimmed with precision and then she took her time memorizing every wicked corner of his mouth.

Liberty accepted a shrimp wrapped in bacon from a passing waiter, then took a bite while her gaze scanned the crowd, noticing the beautiful decorations. A stunning nine-foot Christmas tree stood in one corner with a mountain of gifts underneath.

"What would you like to drink?" Sheyna asked, dragging her attention away.

Liberty took a brief moment to think. "A cosmopolitan if it's not too much trouble."

She winked. "Watch this... Jace, we need a Cosmo over here!"

The dark, handsome man looked over at his wife and grinned. "Coming right up."

A tall gorgeous man with long dreadlocks brushing his shoulders was sitting at the end of the bar and cried, "You don't want him making it! We'll be scraping you off the floor."

Bianca gave a dismissive wave. "Jaden, behave."

Liberty leaned in close to the beauty. "Is that your brother, the one married to the model?"

She nodded. "Yes, Danica's around here ... oh there she is over there with the kids." Liberty looked over at the tall, red-headed beauty, who was bouncing a little girl on her lap. Her features were still flawless as ever.

There was a knock at the door and then a clown and his entourage walked into the house and all the kids started screaming with excitement. The older cousins took the little ones into a room where the party was about to begin.

"Here's your drink."

Startled, Liberty looked up to see Jace standing beside her. Dark mocha skin, sable eyes, the man was so good-looking he took her breath away. There was a seriousness about him that softened every time he looked at Sheyna.

She rushed over as soon as her husband walked away. "Let me know if it's strong because he can be heavy handed with the vodka."

Liberty took a sip and started coughing.

"Told ya!" Jaden said, with a chuckle, as he headed toward the front of the house. "Stick around long enough, you'll learn." He gave a sympathetic look, then went to join the kids.

Sheyna signaled for Liberty to follow. "Come with me." She led her through all the guests. Friendly greetings were called out to Liberty as she passed, making her feel warm and welcomed. She stepped into a huge kitchen with white subway tiles, travertine floors, and white and gray granite. Liberty gasped in awe as she walked over to the massive-sized island and lowered on one of the six barstools. "Your kitchen is beautiful."

Sheyna opened a huge stainless-steel refrigerator then looked over her shoulder and grinned. "Thanks girl. It took almost a year to get it the way I wanted it."

She reached inside, pulled out a Sprite, popped the can then walked over and poured some into her glass. "How's that?"

Liberty sipped and then nodded. "Much better."

"Good, now let me take a seat, because I want to know how you feel about my brother."

♥ ♥ ♥

"That little dude looks just like you."

Darnell nodded with pride. "Yeah he does, doesn't he?"

"How does it feel being a dad?" Jabarie Beaumont asked, sable-colored eyes probing.

He couldn't find the words to describe how it felt knowing he was responsible for teaching his son about life and how to someday be a man. "Dude, it's a lot of pressure," he confessed with a bark of laughter.

Jabarie and Brenna Beaumont had five children and plenty of experience. Darnell couldn't even imagine raising that many, although he had caught himself thinking about having a little girl of his own. He wasn't sure where that ridiculous thought had come from. The last thing he wanted was another baby mama. Although the one he had wasn't so bad.

Once again, he glanced across the room to steal a peek at Liberty. Sheyna had taken her hand and was leading her away. *Probably to pick her brain for information*, he thought with a groan.

"Are you thinking about settling down?" Jabarie's words caused him to swirl around.

"Oh no. I'm not ready for that," he denied and even as he said it it didn't have the conviction it once had. The more time he spent with Chance the more he wanted to be a daily part of his life.

What about Liberty?

He enjoyed being around her too much. He couldn't wait to see her smiling face and just smell the sweet scent that was all her own. But he liked what they had and he didn't want to mess that up by confusing what they had for something it was not.

"Dude, never say never." Jabarie patted him on the back and headed over to stand beside his wife. Darnell watched the way he ran his hand lovingly up and down Brenna's arm, caressing, claiming what was his, and he felt an unfamiliar wave of envy.

As he stood near the Christmas tree, Darnell thought about his parents. Often he'd wondered if his mother had lived would his parents still be together? Sheyna had been too young to remember, but he recalled the nights he heard his parents arguing and the days they went without speaking, with him and Scott passing messages back and forth. But then there were the days they were curled up on the couch together watching a movie, or the cries of joy he used to hear from the other side of the wall at night when he was supposed to be sleeping. He grew up believing marriage was a crazy roller coaster and he just wasn't sure he was up for the emotional toll it took on people. His clients were proof of the stress and agony marriage caused. Nevertheless, that didn't stop him from enjoying being with his son and Liberty.

Darnell looked over at Chance playing with the others like they had been cousins forever, then he strolled toward the kitchen to see what his sister was up to.

He went down the long hall, thumping across the wood floor to the kitchen that was now located in the new addition of the house. As he neared, he heard female chatter and laughter.

"Trust me, it never gets any easier," he heard his

sister say. "It's just after being with the same man for almost a decade you finally get to the point you just throw your hands up and realize you married a nut."

There was more laughter.

"They are all crazy," Jennifer chimed in.

"Well at least that explains it," Zanaa added.

"Honey, it's just getting started. I tried to warn you before you married my bighead brother," Sheyna reminded and then there was more laughter.

"Liberty you've been around my brother long enough. You might want to run while you still can."

With a groan, Darnell pushed open the door. The kitchen grew quiet and then the women looked at him then back at each other and exploded with laughter.

"Did I miss something funny?" he asked sheepishly as he stepped across the room and grabbed a bottle of water from the refrigerator.

Sheyna was eating wings and licking buffalo sauce off her fingers. "Just a little girl talk, that's all," she replied.

Jennifer smiled up at him, and dimples dominated both cheeks. "We're explaining what life is like with a Simmons."

He took another long swallow, then gave a playful groan. "Lib, don't listen to anything they say."

Liberty was sitting at the island with Jennifer. "I don't know," she began. "I'm trying to find out what to expect as Chance gets older. Now I'm a little scared." Her eyes were twinkling with laughter.

And there was that pretty smirk he adored. "I see they've been feeding you lies, which is why I came in here to drag you away before they corrupt you."

His family started talking all at once. Darnell tossed the bottle in the trash then strolled over, took Liberty by the hand and gently yanked her to her feet.

"Dee, we're trying to get to know her!" Zanaa called after him.

"She'll be back later."

Liberty was laughing along with the others. "If I come up missing, you know who to blame," she whispered loudly and then grabbed onto the door frame as if he was taking her against her will.

"Funny." he frowned, then gave her arm a yank and there was more girlish laughter.

"I see you got jokes," Darnell replied as he led her away from the kitchen and down another hallway.

Liberty tilted her head towards his, smiling. "Your family adores you."

He frowned. "So I've heard."

"You were listening?"

He chuckled. "Only the good parts." He led her into a room that stared off at the water.

"Oh this is beautiful," she gasped.

He nodded. "They had it added two years ago."

The room was completely enclosed in glass. Moving over to the window, Liberty stared out onto the sprawling lawn and what looked like a five-car detached garage. Trees lined one side of the property and the lawn sloped down toward the cliff and the ocean below. A white rail fence meandered along the cliff's edge.

"I could spend hours in this room lost in my thoughts."

Darnell moved behind her until his chest was pressed against her back and wrapped his arms around her middle. "What do you think about?"

His body tingled from the contact and ignited a need to protect her from whatever bothered her.

"Life. Where I want to be in five years ..., providing for my son so he can have every possible opportunity in life. Things like that."

"Those are the things I've also been thinking about lately."

Liberty sighed. "I grew up with a father who spent my entire life bitter and blaming me for my mother's death."

At the pain in her voice, Darnell's arms tightened around her.

"He didn't mistreat me, not physically, but he never showed me love. I don't want my son to ever feel that way. And today, being around all of you, I know that he's going to always feel loved and a part of a family."

Gently, Darnell turned Liberty around and stared deeply into her eyes. "Hey," he said making sure he had her attention. "You never have to worry about my son. I will do everything I can to provide him every opportunity or die trying."

A solitary tear rolled down her cheek. "Thank you. There's nothing worse than feeling like you're all alone in the world."

He gave her a soft smile. "You saw all the people in this house. That will never happen. Neither of you will ever have to feel alone ever again." He brushed her cheek. "You're Chance's mother and that makes you family." Tenderly he ran the tip of his finger along the curve of her face and neck.

"Thank you," she whispered.

"If you haven't noticed. I care about you." His voice was raw with emotion. Liberty's eyes widened and when her lips parted in surprise they were too delicious to ignore. Darnell leaned toward her and took her mouth in a possessive kiss.

Her arms came up around his neck and he drew her close into the circle of his hold. Her lips were hot.

When she moaned she lit a fire in the pit of his stomach.

With a groan, his lips traveled across her cheek, ear and down across her neck before turning to her lips again.

Liberty tilted her head back giving him better access to nibble and suck at her tender flesh before he returned to her mouth again. Her lips parted on a gasp and his tongue swooped inside and stroked and teased until she was moaning.

His hands snaked across the curved of her hips along her ass, then across her back. As the kiss increased he came around to stroke the sides of her breasts and she whimpered and arched into his hands.

It was crazy, almost insane. He needed to be inside her, have her feel just how much she meant to him.

"I want you," he whispered.

"And I you," she breathed.

"Come home with me tonight."

She turned her face as if suddenly needing to catch her breath. "No, that would be confusing."

"Then dammit, I'm coming home with you. And don't try and stop me," he growled.

Liberty purred between kisses. "I wouldn't dream of it."

♥ ♥ ♥

It was almost midnight when they made it to the house. Darnell hung the coats in the hall closet then said, "If you don't mind, I'd like to put my son to bed tonight."

Liberty looked at Darnell and nodded. "Sure, go ahead while I take a shower."

"Alright Chance, let's go."

They raced up the stairs like two morons. Shaking

her head she climbed the steps and went into her room. There was no doubt Darnell could handle Chance all by himself.

She shut her bedroom door and removed her clothes as she padded into the bathroom and started the shower. A smile tickled her lips as she thought about the amazing evening they'd had. Darnell had a wonderful family.

And he's not so bad himself.

Liberty drew a shaky breath as she thought about the kiss they had shared in the sunroom and then the affection he had shown throughout the rest of the evening. A kiss here... a caress there. It was enough that Jennifer had pulled her to the side to ask what was going on between the two of them. Liberty had no idea. She knew what she wanted, but Darnell had yet to admit if his feelings had changed. Shaking her head, she pulled the dress over her head. She was getting ahead of herself again and she needed to stay focused and just enjoy the moment no matter how difficult it was. Part of her wanted all or nothing while the rest of her yearned for his touch and was willing to take whatever she could get even if it was just for the moment. And tonight that was exactly what she planned to do.

♥ ♥ ♥

"See you in the morning."

"G'nite Mr. Dee," Chance said and closed his eyes.

Darnell dropped a kiss to his forehead, then returned the book to the shelf and shut the door on his way out. He stood there outside his room, trying to catch his breath.

I'm a father.

Sometimes he had a hard time believing a decision

he had made in college turned out to be the best thing to ever happen to him. And he planned to do everything in his power to always be there for his son.

What about his mother?

He heard humming coming from Liberty's room. The soft melody caused him to smile. Darnell pushed away from the door, and strolled down the hall toward her room and opened the door. As he stepped into the room, he spotted Liberty standing in front of her dresser. All it took was one long look and desire enflamed his mind with reckless wanting.

"Hey," she said as she closed one of the drawers. "Chance all tucked in?"

Darnell nodded and was too afraid to move as he stared at her wearing a see-thru nightgown.

Darnell swore softly under his breath. He wanted to give her pleasure she had never experienced before. He wanted to possess every part of her body even though he knew what they had was temporary. They shared a son. That was one thing no other woman could say.

"Take your hair down," he growled.

He watched as Liberty lifted her hands to her hair, causing her breasts to surge forward against the flimsy material and there was no disguising her hard nipples straining against the nightgown. He groaned. She wasn't the only one turned on. He was aroused and erect, straining to be unzipped.

As she pulled out pins and her spiraled hair sprung free into that moppy-style he loved so much, he was no longer able to resist the need to touch her. Pushing the door shut with a click, he closed the distance between them.

Liberty dragged in a breath and tried to stay perfectly still as he lifted the gown slowly over her head, his fingers grazing her skin. With the briefest touch, his penis throbbed. And the sight of her naked from the waist up…, he tossed the gown aside and drew in a long shaky breath. Liberty was beautiful and sexy and he wanted her. He wanted her so damn bad he was willing to beg if he had to.

Lust burned from his eyes as he took his time devouring every luscious inch of her. Large round breasts tipped by hard chocolate nipples. Soft smooth, butter-brown skin covered a body with enough curves to cause a traffic jam. Then there was her small waist and the cute belly button.

"Now take off your panties," he ordered and Liberty dragged them down her thighs, stepped out and tossed the pair onto the floor.

"Don't move. I want to look at you." He took in every luscious curve of her body and shook his head. His eyes traveled down to a bush of curly brown hair that had been perfectly trimmed just enough for him to see the hood that covered that hard nub.

"You're so beautiful." Itching to touch her, Darnell lifted his hand to her breasts and caressed her. A whimper escaped her lips that made his loins heat.

"You like that? Huh? Talk to me Lib," he said seductively.

"Yes," she began. "I like that," she whispered and her eyelids rolled. "I have no control when you touch me like that."

The sight of her naked, standing in front of him, tore the breath from his lungs. Her breathing increased, and her chest rose and fell, lifting her breasts into his hand.

"Look at me," he ordered, quietly.

Liberty opened her eyes.

"I don't want no mistake as to who's touching

you." He fondled her breasts as he spoke.

"You're embarrassing me," she whispered.

"Sweetheart you have absolutely nothing to be embarrassed about," he growled as shots of pleasure surged to his stomach. "Your breasts are perfect, you got ass for days and your pussy.... Oooh-weee!" he howled, causing her to giggle. "I'm serious, you are so fine, I can't keep my hands off of you." As he spoke he pinched her nipples. Her lips parted, but no words came out. The arousal on her face turned him on in ways he couldn't even begin to put to words.

Licking his lips, Darnell drew her closer, then took a nipple between his lips. Liberty gasped and a sweet aching need to possess her surged down between his thighs. He suckled, tongued her taut peak, and groaned.

Jesus, she tasted good!

♥ ♥ ♥

Her nipple slipped from his mouth as Darnell moved across her chest to the other one. Goodness! She didn't have the strength to speak. All she could do was make little mewling sounds.

"I think I've found your spot," he murmured. "Your left nipple is your trigger point."

Damn, he was too smart for his own good and attentive too, she noted. Most men took forever, if at all, to find out how aroused she became by just simply playing with her left nipple.

While Darnell fondled her breasts, he slid the other hand gently down along her stomach. "And you're even softer here." His fingers crept through the dark nest of curls and she heard a low moan escape her throat.

He raised his gaze to hers. "Babe, open your legs

for me." His voice had hardened to a command.

With a shaky breath, Liberty spread her feet.

Darnell's long fingers slid between her thighs and began stroking her clit that caused her hips to rock. As he stroked her, the pleasure grew into a powerful throbbing that had her straining to get as close to his hand as possible.

"You like this, don't you?" he asked as he penetrated her with his finger.

"Yes… oh yes," she panted and brought her hands to his shoulders to steady herself before her knees buckled.

"Keep your eyes opened. That's it … I love the way you look when you're ready to come."

Coming was definitely brewing, she thought and rocked her pussy along the length of his long fingers, but no matter how fast she moved she was unable to relieve the pressure building between her thighs.

"Yeah baby, just like that. Ride my hand," he moaned and cupped her ass with his other hand and pushed her forward for deeper penetration. "Tell me you like it," he commanded.

"Yes," she rasped. "Yes. I like it. Please don't stop." It was all she could manage. She buried her face at the base of his neck while she clutched at his shoulders.

His fingers pumped harder, while his thumb rubbed her clit until she screamed. Her hips kept pace, rocking against his hand until he grabbed her thigh and raised her leg alongside his.

"Please," she begged.

"Say my name," he growled. "Say, please make me come Darnell."

If that's what it took to end the agony and give her what she wanted, so be it. "Dee… Please… make me come."

While she whimpered and begged for release, Darnell slid another finger inside her, surging in and out while stroking her clit with his thumb. Within moments she exploded, crying out his name before he covered her mouth, silencing her with his. He continued to pump his fingers in and out until the tremors and her breathing slowed.

When she finally opened her eyes, she found Darnell watching her. Her leg was still up against his body and his fingers were still buried between her folds of her swollen pussy.

"You come?" he asked, lips twitching with humor.

"You know I did." A soft moan caught in her throat as Liberty lowered her leg and released him.

"Now it's your turn," she replied. "Lie down on the bed."

He chuckled. "I got a better idea. Take my hand." Darnell led her over to a chaise lounge she had positioned in front of a window. "Now stand right there."

Liberty gripped the chair and waited as he removed his jeans followed by his boxers and tossed them in her line of vision so she could see what he had removed. His shirt followed. Anticipation sliced through her as she waited for him to rip open a condom and sheath himself. His breath was hot on her neck and then she felt his erection press against her ass. Liberty gazed out between the curtains and moaned with satisfaction when Darnell dipped his head to nuzzle the side of her neck. She felt a tingling sensation starting from her head and worked down to all her intimate parts before reaching her toes. In a few moments, Darnell was going to be inside her again.

"Now I want you to close your eyes," he began in a low voice. "I want you to feel everything I'm about to do to you."

Liberty lowered her eyelids and braced herself for what was about to come.

He pressed his body against hers, his erection pulsing against her. His hands came around and cupped her breasts, thumbs rubbed over her nipples and the sensitive peaks tingled into hard points.

"Spread your legs," he whispered into her ear.

She parted her thighs and felt his erection between the cheeks of her ass. His lips grazed her neck and shoulder causing goose bumps to pop on her skin, making her shake.

"I'm going to make you beg before I give you what you want."

She had a feeling it wouldn't be long before she'd be pleading. Darnell's fingers were all over her. He was stroking her breasts, tasting her neck, and his cock nudged her inner thighs in a teasing motion that made a moan spill from her lips.

"You like that?" he teased.

"Yes," she moaned again.

Darnell's hand slid from her breasts, down across her belly, then down through the curls at her apex. She hissed in a long breath as his fingers traveled lower until they parted her plump, intimate folds. With a whimper her hips bucked upward against his hand in a plea for release. How was it possible that she was desperate to come again? His teeth nibbled at her shoulder as he slipped a finger inside her. She exhaled and squeezed around the invasion.

"You're so wet."

And she was about to get even wetter, she thought as her body heated. She was burning with anticipation. "Please," she begged.

"Please what?" His thumb caressed the hard bud

with a steady rhythm, then he stopped only to start again. Teasing and making her want him.

"Make me come," she whimpered.

He lightly chuckled. "The next time you come, it will be while I'm inside of you, but not until you scream for me to take you."

His knee nudged her thighs further apart and then he plunged two fingers inside, pumping in and out in a vigorous rhythm that had her rocking her hips to meet him. His lips were nibbling at her neck while his thumb continued to tease her pulsing clit.

"Please, Dee!" she cried. "I need you inside me now! I'm begging you!"

And then his fingers slipped out and he was bending her lower over the chair. He slammed his cock inside her with one hard push that caused her to cry out in pleasure. "Yes!"

Her breast swayed, as her hips rocked back against him. He pounded his cock into her over and over. A climax hit her and even then he still didn't slow. She was sobbing and crying out his name, the intensity was too much and yet she didn't want him to stop. She wished he never had to stop as one wave of ecstasy after another washed over her. His penis was so hard and he was pulling back and burying himself again so deep he grazed her g-spot over and over, inch by luscious inch teasing her so that she came again and again.

"Dee... don't... stop... please!" she cried with pleasure because she didn't know what she wanted anymore. For him to stop. For him not to. It was so intense and yet it felt so good. And when her legs felt ready to give out, Darnell finally let go and exploded deep inside of her. Liberty sobbed with joy. His hands were at her waist, stroking her until he was spent and her breathing had slowed.

"Come on, babe. Let's get some rest before round two." He then lifted her up in his arms and carried her over to the bed.

Chapter Thirteen

For more reasons than one, Liberty was looking forward to the holiday season. She and Chance would stay with Darnell Christmas Eve and then spend Christmas with his father and Jennifer. Afterwards, they'd planned a sleigh ride with Sheyna and her family.

It was starting to feel natural being together. They enjoyed the same tastes in music, loved to disagree about who was the best team in the NFL, and he adored their son. She couldn't imagine that life could be this way with a man. They laughed and talked several times throughout the day. Darnell called her when the judge dismissed a custody case for a father who had been falsely accused of abusing his son. They went out and celebrated, before returning to her house, where they made love the rest of the night.

"You look happy," Cash said while they were Christmas shopping at Macy's.

Sometimes she's just too observant for her own good.

Liberty shrugged a shoulder as if it was no big deal while trying to downplay how good she actually felt. There was no way she was ready to admit who or what was responsible for that smile. "I'm always happy this time of year."

Of course her friend wasn't buying it. "Uh-uh, you're extra happy this season. I bet Darnell has something to do with that," Cash decided with a calculative grin.

Liberty shook her head as they stepped onto the escalator toward the men's department upstairs. "You are too much, you know that?"

Laughing, she shook her head. "That's why you like me, remember?"

"No, I like you because if I didn't you wouldn't have any friends," she said matter-of-factly even though it was far from the truth. Cash was so popular at the hospital almost everyone knew her and even asked for her by name.

The honey-blonde beauty shot her an exasperated look. "Quit changing the subject. What's going on between the two of you?"

As she stepped off the escalator, Liberty turned away from her probing eyes. "Who says anything is going on?"

Cash rushed to her side, high-heeled boots clicking. "Because you asked me to help you shop for *him* a gift. I think that says it all."

Still avoiding eye contact, Liberty stopped to browse a clearance rack. "I figured I should get Darnell something. It's the least I can do, considering Chance and I are staying with him Christmas Eve," she added as if an afterthought.

"Oh my goodness! Girlfriend, you've been holding out on me!" Cash's eyes were wide as she shuffled quickly around a display of Sean John designer sweaters. "You're getting it on with your baby's daddy?"

Liberty made a face. Cash knew she had never been fond of that phrase. "If you're asking if we're having sex the answer is yes."

She squealed even louder this time. "I knew it!"

"You knew what?"

Cash sniffed. "That the two of you would get together."

Liberty gave a dismissive smile and faked a frown so Cash wouldn't be able to read her expression. If Cash knew what had been going on between the two of them she would never be able to get her to let up.

Ready to change the subject, she browsed a rack and reached for a blue cable knit sweater, when Cash asked, "So you're saying it isn't a relationship?"

She wasted no time shaking her head. "No not at all." Even though deep down she wished there was something defined going on, she wasn't ready yet to share that even with her best friend. "We're just enjoying each other."

Cash made a face. "Enjoying? Sounds like a lot more going on than that."

"We're—"

She held up a hand. "And don't say you're doing it for Chance because it has gone beyond that. The two of you could have just talked, took the blood tests and mutually decided on the amount of time Darnell got to spend with him. You and I both know it's more than that."

Yes, even her heart said it was much more. She just didn't want to admit it because then she would be setting herself up for heartbreak. *Darnell doesn't do commitment. Darnell doesn't do relationships.* She chanted it at least a half dozen times a day.

"We're enjoying the moment. No promises," Liberty explained.

Cash dropped a hand to her waist with a concerned look. "I just hope no one gets hurt."

So do I, she thought with a deep sigh.

Chapter Fourteen

"Mommy is Santa here yet?" Chance asked for the umpteenth time.

She smiled. "Not yet, now eat your peas."

"But why not?" He made a show of pouting at the table.

Liberty tried to keep a straight face. His was so impatient. *I wonder who he gets that from?* "Because it's not morning. You have to go to sleep first, remember?"

"Can I go to bed now?"

She shook her head. "Not until you eat those peas."

Chance then started shoveling food into his mouth so fast, Liberty started laughing. "Silly, slow down before you choke!"

It had been a wonderful day. She had closed 24/7 *Fitness* at three o'clock, then swung by the house long enough to load the SUV with her things. She retrieved Chance from the child development center and they arrived at Darnell's house by five. Remembering he had to meet another attorney for dinner, he had left a key under the mat. Liberty unloaded her vehicle then whipped up something quick for dinner. She and Chance ate while he chatted nonstop about Santa coming to the house.

"And don't forget you have to put out the milk and cookies," she reminded.

"Oh yeah!" he shrieked and the grin on his face

was so priceless.

After dinner, Liberty followed Chance upstairs for his bath. They were just coming down to make hot cocoa when Darnell arrived looking impeccable in an expensive tailored suit and leather loafers. *Sinfully sexy as always*.

"Yo! Santa been here yet?" Darnell bellowed as he walked through the door.

"No silly!" Chance said and squealed with laughter when Darnell scooped him into his arms, calling himself the Tickle Monster.

While the two of them horsed around, Liberty strolled back to the kitchen and put on the tea kettle, then reached for the sheet of precut cookies shaped like trees and stuck them into the preheated oven.

By the time Darnell changed into jeans and a black t-shirt, and he and Chance came racing into the kitchen, she was pouring hot water into all of the mugs. Liberty carried Chance's over to the table.

"How was your day?" Darnell asked, and while Chance was plopping marshmallows into his mug, he gave Liberty a long lingering kiss on the mouth.

When Darnell finally came up for air, Liberty breathed and replied, "We shut down at noon, had our office Christmas party and then I let everyone go home." Liberty carried her mug over and sat at the table. Darnell grabbed his and lowered onto the seat across from her. He was sitting so close she smelled the intoxicating scent of his skin that was uniquely male and all Darnell.

"I had a good day. One of my cases settled out of court," he said conversationally.

"That's a good thing, right?"

"Definitely," he murmured lazily. "Not that I don't mind the billable hours, but the more my clients can work out on their own the better."

They sipped and chatted until Liberty pulled the cookies out of the oven. Darnell then helped Chance spread sprinkles on top. As soon as they were cool, she reached for a spatula and placed them on a plate then prepared another. As she put them in the oven, she watched while Chance carried the saucer of cookies and a small cup of milk to the family room for Santa Claus. She was tingling inside.

It was truly starting to feel like Christmas.

Hours later, Liberty was loading the last glass in the dishwasher when Darnell came down stairs. "He's sound asleep," he announced. Stepping over to her, he dropped a kiss to her lips. "Come on. It's Santa time."

He took Liberty's hand and led her into the laundry room with its stainless-steel front-load washer and dryer, utility sink, and a long table for folding. As she watched with curiosity, Darnell pulled out a key and unlocked the closet door. She drew in a breath at what she saw inside. The space was stacked high with toys.

Liberty gave him a narrowed-eye look. "I don't remember us buying all those gifts." Last week Darnell had picked her up at lunch for a little Christmas shopping.

Laughing, he gave Liberty an irresistible boyish smirk. "Well... let's just say Santa swung by and he and his elves dropped off a few more gifts."

She laughed and shook her head. "I'm warning you. You're spoiling him."

Darnell scratched his ear and for the first time, he looked slightly sheepish. "This is my first Christmas as a dad. Let me enjoy it."

Liberty nodded. Darnell was right. She'd had a

four-year head start and had no business taking this moment away from him.

Together they pulled everything out the closet and began carrying the toys into the family room surrounding the tree. She smiled when she spotted the shiny new bike. Chance had outgrown his tricycle and was ready for training wheels.

Liberty rolled it into the room and found Darnell stacking logs in the fireplace. "I figured I'd build us a fire."

"Good idea," she said and wheeled the bike under the tree.

"How are we going to do this?"

She whipped around, brow arched, unsure who or what he was talking about? "What do you mean?"

His hot, bold gaze met hers. "I mean, getting everything ready for Christmas morning. Do you wrap all the presents?"

His eyes were burning with the curiosity of an anxious child and it warmed her heart to see Darnell so passionate about being a student of Chance's past. He could have come up with his own ideas, and yet, instead he was willing to stick with tradition.

"Well," she began, and took a seat on the leather sectional. "I usually wrap a few of the gifts. Although as many as Chance has this year, we could start our own toy store," she added with a sweep of the hand.

Darnell simply chuckled and lit the starter log.

"Each year I always make sure one of his gifts comes from his mother, not Santa Claus, and then there are always gifts under the tree from Cash as well."

Darnell nodded and took one last look at the fire then rose from the floor in a fluid motion. "Good idea. I'll make sure I put my name on a few gifts."

Stretching her legs out in front of her, she agreed.

"I want him to know it's the season of giving and everything doesn't come from Santa."

"I agree," he replied. Darnell stroked his chin between his thumb and forefinger as he gazed provocatively at her. Liberty felt her nipples tingling under the intensity.

"We better get this over with," she mumbled and unfolded her body from the sectional, practically racing into the laundry room.

They went back to unloading the closet. By then the fire was roaring and spreading warmth throughout the room. Once they were done, Liberty retrieved her storage container filled with decorations she had carried in from her vehicle. She wrapped a new Power Ranger action figure in candy cane wrapping paper. It was a gift from Cash. And then she put a big red bow on the shiny new bike. It would be a gift from her.

Darnell had tuned onto a radio station that was playing Christmas music twenty-four hours a day until New Year's Eve. Toni Braxton was singing, "Snowflakes of Love."

While she and Darnell worked together to assemble everything under the sun, Liberty caught herself watching him. *Why'd he have to be so fine?* And then there was the cozy family feeling creeping through her veins. How in the world was she supposed to spend Christmas with a man who threw her equilibrium all out of whack? One touch, a single look, and sizzling heat pooled between her thighs. She was a goner. And it wasn't fair. After all these years since her husband's death, she had finally found everything a woman could ever want in a man and yet he wanted no part of a relationship. *Just my luck.*

"Did you grow up believing in Santa?" she asked, desperate to think of something else.

Darnell rocked back on his heels and grinned at the question. "I believed in Santa Claus until I was nine."

"What happened?"

"My father had fallen asleep and forgot to shut his closet door. I happened to walk in there to ask him a question and spotted the Batman cave I'd been begging my Dad for, peeking out from behind his clothes. Once I saw it under the tree the next morning, I knew then there was no Santa."

But at least for a while he got to dream and believe, she thought with a sad smile.

They laughed and talked, then drank egg nog while wrapping presents. By the time Darnell remembered he'd forgotten something and raced up stairs, Liberty's entire body was tingling with want and she was relieved for a few brief moments to get her head on right. Tonight was one evening she would never forget, but the last thing she wanted was to make more of the evening than it really was.

She went back to wrapping gifts and hummed along with Whitney Houston as she sang, "Joy to the World." She wasn't sure how long Darnell had been standing over her before she noticed him and flinched.

"You scared me!" she cried and brought a hand to her chest.

"Sorry," Darnell replied and then his lips touched hers. By the time he pulled back, her pulse had slowed and that's when she noticed the package in his hand. Liberty eyes searched his beneath those incredible lashes.

"Merry Christmas, Lib."

His voice sent heat coursing through her causing her words to come out in a gasp, "You didn't have to get me a gift." She knew it was Christmas and yet she hadn't expected to receive anything.

"Yes, I did. Now here… take it."

She was still holding her breath when she took the box from Darnell's hand. "Okay, but wait a sec." She scrambled to her feet then moved over to the storage container and fished around at the bottom, and when she found what she was looking for, Liberty swung around and shoved a beautifully wrapped gift toward him.

"Merry Christmas."

Stunned, Darnell held his hands up and shook his head. "Oh no, you've given me enough already."

"It's Christmas." When he hesitated, she added with a wink, "You better take it, or else …" She wagged her eyebrows suggestively.

"Well, in that case…" he conceded. "Thank you." Darnell took the box from her hands then lowered on the floor in front of the fire. "Okay, you first," he urged, his voice a low, husky command.

Laughing, Liberty lowered beside him, then ripped open the package. What she found inside the box caused her lips to part in surprise. She couldn't believe it. "How did you know?" she squealed.

Darnell gave a slow, wicked smile that made her toes curl as he replied, "A little birdy told me."

"Uh-huh. A *Cash* bird," she said with a smirk and clutched the navy blue designer purse to her chest. She loved surprises. "Thank you so much." It was the same one she had admired at Jennie's Couture. "Now, it's your turn."

He grinned. "Okay."

While he tore away the wrapping, Liberty nibbled on the inside of her lip, hoping he liked the gift.

As soon as Darnell opened the box, he exhaled sharply. "Wow!" And then other than Michael Jackson singing about catching Mama kissing Santa Claus, silence filled the room. Darnell had grown quiet enough for her to hear the rapid beating of her heart

"I wanted to share some special moments of Chance's life with you," she explained.

He stared down at the matted picture frame that showcased twelve, three-by-five photographs of Chance, starting from the day he was born until his fourth birthday. A muscle ticked at his jaw and then she saw wave of emotions flickering in his gaze that brought tears to her eyes.

"Thank you so much, Lib," Darnell said softly and then coughed as if he had something in his throat.

"You're welcome." Liberty leaned forward and wrapped her arms around Darnell's neck, planting a kiss on his soft, sensual lips. "Hey, how about some more hot cocoa?" she asked, trying to lighten the mood again.

A smile curled his lips as he said, "I'll even have marshmallows." He kissed her twice more, then brought Liberty to her feet and led her into the kitchen with a hand to her waist that made her skin quiver.

They took a break, laughing and talking at the table while having cookies and hot cocoa. After eating almost a dozen cookies, they went back to work, assembling a toy train set. Once they got it running around the track, they were finally finished.

"Don't forget Santa's milk and cookies," she reminded.

"Oh yeah." Darnell walked over to the coffee table, ate two of the cookies and took a single bite out of the third then poured out the milk so it would look as if it had been drank. Then they took a step back and stared at their handiwork.

"I think the stage has been set. What about you?" Liberty asked with a hand planted at her hip.

Darnell was nodding and grinning at the same time. "Babe, I think we did good."

"And not a second too soon." Liberty flicked her wrist and glanced down at her watch. "It's after midnight and officially Christmas."

"Merry Christmas," Darnell murmured and dragged her in for a long, searing kiss that sent heat rushing to her belly before she pulled away and groaned.

"We better get this mess cleaned up."

Reluctantly, he agreed.

She cleaned up all the wrapping paper while Darnell put the fire out and then they carried all the trash out to the garage. She was exhausted and happy. "Finally," she breathed.

"Santa's going to be coming soon, so little girl, it's time for bed." Before she could object, Darnell scooped Liberty into his arms and carried her up to his room.

♥ ♥ ♥

Darnell couldn't keep his hands off of her.

The entire evening while getting ready for Christmas he'd been waiting and wanting to hold her in his arms again. And now the time had come.

While he sucked on her bottom lip, his hands roamed over the curves of her body.

"I think someone is horny," Liberty purred.

He growled. "I am. It's been a long week." He cupped her ass and pulled her closer so she could feel his dick pulsing against her belly. "That's what you do to me."

A moan tore from her throat. He loved that sound. Leaning forward he nuzzled his nose along her cheek, inhaling the unique feminine scent of her butter-brown skin.

His hand came up to cup her breasts. "Your nipples are hard," he whispered.

She laughed. "No they aren't."

"Oh Lib, yes they are." He released a few buttons until the tops of her breasts were exposed then dipped his head, nibbling and sucking, driving himself insane.

"Oh, Darnell!" she cried.

Nothing had ever tasted so good. And her moans were so arousing he was overwhelmed with the need to be buried inside her. Reaching down between her thighs, he cupped her, stroking across the crotch of her jeans, relishing in the heat and dampness he felt there.

"Get undressed," he commanded, then released her.

While he unbuttoned his shirt, he watched as she shrugged down her jeans and tossed them and her blouse, followed by a lace bra over onto a chair.

Mesmerized, he stared at the rounded curves of her ass covered in black satin. Darnell swallowed hard as he admired a stomach that was so flat it was hard to imagine she had once carried his child inside. He unbuckled his jeans while staring at the view in front of him. It didn't disappoint.

As soon as his jeans were off, he took her hand, pulling her close, the rapid breathing was arousing, the hungry look in her eyes was almost enough to make his legs buckle. But it also made him ache with a throbbing hardness deep in his gut until he had to take her, had to be inside her warm and wet body.

Darnell ran a thumb down along her back. Her skin, warm and so soft his head was swimming, his desire so intense he could barely breathe. He took her mouth in another deep kiss and he felt her body relax, giving into the passion that flared so naturally between them. How was it possible that he was with a woman that he just couldn't seem to get enough of? He felt a sense of awe that she was there with him, and a strong need to please her.

Darnell shoved her panties to the side and teased around her clitoris. His hard-on was pressing against her thigh, urging him to slip inside her panties and take Liberty from behind. "You should have taken these off," he said.

"And that would take the fun outta *you* taking them off me."

His fingers stroked her swollen folds causing her to quiver. "You're so wet," he announced then fisted the crotch and ripped the material away from her body. "Ah," he moaned. "That was fun."

She giggled and slipped her arms around his neck, then pulled his head down pressing her lips to his.

While his tongue danced with hers, Darnell slipped a finger inside her wetness, and he felt her pussy clamping down around him. Her head dipped and her fingers gripped his shoulders. Drawing back slightly, he gazed at the fire burning in her eyes. "Talk to me, babe."

Liberty's thighs rocked forward riding the length of his finger. "I love the way... you make me feel... with your mouth—Ooh!... and your hands." She managed between breaths while he rolled his thumb around her swollen nub. Everything about her was vibrating with arousal.

Lowering his head again he kissed the swell of her breasts trailing his tongue across her nipple before drawing it into his mouth. She moaned, arched toward his lips while still grinding against his finger as if desperate to come.

It was his job to make that happen.

Dropping to his knees, his tongue followed the

descent down below her belly. A throaty moan jerked from her throat as he grazed across her soft curls and then between her legs, forcing her to part her thighs and allow him room to explore.

"Babe, spread them just a little bit more. *Aaah*, that's it."

Darnell parted her folds, then snaked out his tongue, taking a taste. She trembled, as he held onto her waist pinning her in place for his leisurely assault.

"Oh!" Liberty quivered and shook beneath his tongue. Her hands were planted on his shoulder.

"Are you watching me eat your pussy?" he asked.

"Yes," she panted.

Looking up the long length of her smooth, brown, naked body to the most amazing breasts he'd ever caressed, Darnell smiled at her. "Good, I want you to see everything I'm doing to you." He told her and then tongued her clit.

♥ ♥ ♥

Oh God!

Darnell drew her clit into his mouth and sucked. Liberty tried to evade his tongue, but he was strong and she had nothing to hold onto but his shoulders. She moaned and flinched and tried to push him away but he didn't stop.

"Tonight I want you to beg for me to fuck you."

She was certain that wouldn't be too much longer, especially how good his tongue felt. Darnell had the ability to do all kind of interesting little things, moving slow, sucking with his tongue, stroking with his fingers.

He was still holding her firmly in place and though she felt her legs ready to collapse, she was too close to an orgasm to beg him to stop. His tongue was delicious, his fingers confident and arousing. The feeling that was building was so erotic, she couldn't bring herself to stop him.

"Lie down," she heard Darnell say and discovered somehow he had backed her toward the couch in the sitting room. Grateful, she fell onto the cushions.

Once again his head was buried, her legs he draped over his shoulders, spreading her wide while his tongue stroked her over and over. Liberty whimpered and moaned and then with his fingers, he parted her folds, reached forward and sucked the swollen nub into his mouth.

"Dee!" Liberty cried as she squirmed on the couch.

"Yes, Lib? Tell me."

"It's so good... It's *sooo* good," she chanted.

Her breathing became labored and ragged and she tried to pull away, but his mouth was everywhere, teeth grazing her thigh, tongue assaulting her clit. Cries spilled from her mouth. "Please ..., I'm ready... fuck me!" Her voice sounded desperate and she didn't care about anything except Darnell being inside of her again. Instead he continued to eat her out, this time becoming almost rough.

Just the way she liked it.

She spread her legs even farther apart. "Don't stop!" she whimpered. "Don't you dare stop!"

"I wouldn't dream of it," he said in a sinful voice that made her shudder. And within moments an orgasm tore through her.

"*Yessss! Yessss!*" His tongue continued to stroke her while she shuddered and moaned. And when her breathing finally slowed, he drew back, still resting on his knees.

"Oh my," she whispered between breaths.

Darnell rose, and she lay there, admiring his

beautiful body as he finished undressing. After reaching into a drawer, he rolled on a condom, then strolled back to the couch and wasted no time wrapping her legs around his waist and slid inside her. He didn't wait for her body to accommodate. He didn't pump slowly. Instead he buried himself deep. Liberty didn't stop him, instead, her body savored the welcome feeling of being joined as one again.

"Bring your knees to your chest," he commanded. Once her feet were planted on the cushion, leaving her pussy spread wide, he was pumping in and out.

I must be dreaming. It felt so good, Liberty never wanted him to stop. It could have gone on forever and it still wouldn't have been enough.

She felt her inner muscles quivering and edging him on. Darnell held onto the head of the couch and threw his hip back then sank into her again and again. Every muscles in her body tightened. "I'm coming!" she screamed and then an orgasm raced through her.

Her body jerked and she whimpered until she felt him shudder, then he moaned against her lips. He finally collapsed on the couch and grabbed her arm dragging her down onto the floor until she was lying across his chest. While they lay there, his hand caressed her spine, he kissed her forehead. Liberty sighed and wished the moment would never end.

But she knew there was no such thing as happy endings.

Chapter Fifteen

"Mommy, Santa came! Mommy!"

"Huh?" she mumbled as she rolled over on the bed.

"Mommy, get up!"

Slowly she raised her heavy eyelids to find herself in the guest bedroom with Chance standing over her with that goofy grin on his face. She smiled. "Good morning. Merry Christmas."

"Merry Christmas. Mommy, Santa came!" Chance's eyes were wide with excitement.

"He did? Wow!" she said playing along. Quickly, she flung the covers back and padded over to the chair beside the door and retrieved her robe. "Sweetheart, give me a minute and I'll be right down."

"'Kay." He dashed out the room and down the stairs. Smiling, she slipped her arms into the micro-suede robe and tied it around her waist, then moved to the bathroom down the hall. Liberty stepped over to the sink and turned on the faucet. While the water ran she stared at her reflection. Last night was one to remember.

They had made love until the wee hours of the morning, then she had crawled from underneath his sleeping body and moved down the hall to climb into the queen-sized bed in the spare bedroom. Immediately she had missed the comfort of lying in Darnell's arms but she didn't want to confuse Chance when he awakened to find his parents sleeping in the same bed.

A few minutes later she came padding downstairs and into the kitchen. Chance was seated at the small table in the breakfast nook shoveling cereal quickly into his mouth. Her eyes shifted over to Darnell who was sitting across from him. Her heart banged in her chest. He looked handsome even in a gray t-shirt and black sweat pants. His feet was bare. As soon as he spotted her, his eyes lit up.

"Good morning." He rose from the table and walked over toward the counter. "You want some coffee?"

"Please," she replied and suddenly felt nervous. "Chance, you ready to open your presents?"

His mouth was too stuffed to talk so he simply nodded.

Darnell place a cup in the Keurig and pressed the button. Instantly the water began to heat. Swinging around, he rested his hip against the island. "I told him we had to wait for you so he's been anxious."

"How long have you both been up?" she asked combing her fingers through her hair.

He looked down at his watch. "Maybe about thirty minutes." He then stepped closer and whispered, "I didn't like waking up alone."

Tilting her head, she gazed up at him. "Is that so?"

"Yep, I had plans on how I wanted to start my Christmas morning."

Gazing at him, she tried not to think about what he meant. All of the possibilities that sprang to her mind had her body pulsing in remembrance. Before she had a chance to recover, Darnell tugged her closer, and pressed a warm, gentle kiss to her lips.

"Good morning," he purred then pulled away, still

grinning at her.

Her shoulders sagged with relief and the nervous feeling ceased. Somehow his kisses had a way of making her feel that everything was going to be alright between them.

He winked, then padded barefoot over to the Keurig and reached for her mug then carried it over to the island. "Cream, sugar?"

"I'm ready!" Chance slipped off the chair and scurried into the family room.

"Hold that thought." She looked over at Darnell. "I guess it's show time."

"I wouldn't miss it for the world." He brought a hand to the small of her back and ushered her into the family room. The feel of his hip brushing against hers made her feel all warm and fuzzy inside. This was what family was like.

I could get used to this.

Last night had been the most recent example of how good they were together. But no matter how great today would be, she was crazy about a man she had no future with. Letting herself love him even just a little was going to be a problem if she didn't stay focused.

The next hour was what she had always dreamed Christmas to be. Darnell pulled out a camera and shot dozens of photographs while Chance ripped open one beautifully wrapped gift followed by another. He was so excited about finding everything he had asked for from Santa under the tree.

"You're spoiling him," she scolded.

Darnell simply shrugged. "You ain't seen nothing yet. Wait until we go to my Dad's house. He and Sheyna are planning on making up four years of Christmas."

Liberty gave a playful groan. "You're creating a

little monster."

Laughing he moved over to the couch and flopped down beside her. "One of the joys of being a parent is being able to spoil your child." He reached over for her hands and laced his long fingers with hers. "Like I told you, my son will never want for anything."

"You just remember that when he starts acting out," she teased.

"Trust me. I believe in spoiling a child, but I don't have no problems laying down the hammer." He balled his fist and started playfully punching her in the arms sending her into a fit of laughter that ended with him drawing her close and kissing her lips.

"Come on. Let's eat while he's entertaining himself," he suggested.

Once they were back in the kitchen, he nuked her coffee and pointed to the cream and sugar on the counter. Liberty poured a heaping spoon of sugar into her mug then moved over to the island and climbed onto one of the wrought iron stools.

"What was Christmas like when you were a child?" he asked as pulled out the bacon and eggs from the refrigerator.

Liberty took a sip from her mug as she remembered her holidays growing up. "Sometimes we had a tree, other years my father said it was a waste of money. I always got something, but I was taught there was no such thing as Santa Claus and since he was such a bah-humbug the holidays were never special."

"Did you have any other family?"

She shook her head. "A few older distant cousins. Dad was an only child. His parents died when he was young and my mother spent her entire life in foster care so she never knew her real family." Liberty noticed the sympathy in his eyes and immediately she shrugged. She had stopped feeling sorry for herself years ago when she decided to create her own happy memories. "And that is why the Christmas season is so special to me."

Darnell gave her a warm and irresistible grin. "Hopefully, we can make this one to remember."

He had no idea how memorable this year would be not only for Chance but for her as well.

"How did you learn to cook?" she asked, changing the subject.

He cracked six eggs into a bowl and stirred. "Well, Dad was a lousy cook," he began with a laugh. "Sheyna tried to do the best she could and Scott could barely boil water. I figured I better learn how to cook or starve so I started reading my mother's cookbooks, and found out I was pretty good at it."

"Was your mother a good cook?"

His eyes twinkled and the far-off look said he was lost in thought. "Mom was amazing in the kitchen. We would wake up on Christmas, smelling cookies baking and bacon frying…" Briefly, he dropped his head and took a moment to pull it together. "Yeah, she was great."

"You're lucky," she whispered, and he looked up at her and they shared a smile.

While he made breakfast, they chatted about the plans for the day. Chance came peddling around and around into the kitchen on his new bicycle.

Within a few minutes Darnell had carried over two plates of eggs and bacon to the oak table in the breakfast nook. While they ate, Liberty stared out the window as the snowflakes began to swirl.

"What's the weather today?" she asked while munching on a slice of bacon.

"The weather man forecasted another four or five

inches of snow."

"Perfect." She grinned. Nothing was better than snow on Christmas day.

♥ ♥ ♥

It snowed heavily the rest of the day. They made it to Darnell's parents' house and spent an amazing day surrounded by family. There were gifts piled high under the tree for all of them, especially for JJ and Chance. Most of the afternoon there was a lump in his throat.

Family.

Every time he looked over at Liberty sitting at the kitchen table with Sheyna and Jennifer, he couldn't help but to also consider her part of the family. He even caught himself imagining her sitting at the table, stomach swollen with child. With two boys, the Simmons now needed a little girl. He could see a beautiful baby with Liberty's wild curly hair, chocolate eyes and smooth butter-brown skin.

"What's on your mind?" he heard Scott say, cutting into his thoughts.

Darnell shook off the images and looked over at his brother sitting in the big arm chair in his father's living room. "Nothing."

Scott's brow raised. "You said nothing but yet I've been talking to you for the last few minutes and you've been somewhere else."

"Just enjoying the day," he replied then leaned forward and grabbed another Christmas cookie from a plate at the center of the coffee table.

"I think you're enjoying playing house more than you care to admit."

He chuckled. "I'm not playing house."

"Then what would you call it? You're spending the

holiday with your son and his mother. And I see the way you keep looking at her." Scott shook his head. "You've finally been bitten."

"Nah," he scowled. "We're just sharing the holiday. Lib doesn't have a family of her own so I invited her to spend it with ours." He shrugged. "Nothing wrong with that."

Scott shook his head again and frowned. "You are in denial."

Darnell disagreed. They were both caught up in the holiday spirit and once the weekend was over things would be back to normal.

"Yeah okay. We'll see," his brother mumbled.

After dinner they all bundled up and headed to downtown Main Street to listen to Christmas carols and to take a sleigh ride. Darnell cuddled under the blanket with Liberty in his arms. Chance rode in the sleigh with JJ and his parents.

"Are you enjoying yourself?" he asked as the horse started a slow trot.

Her head was back against his chest and she looked up at him, eyes wide with childlike excitement. "This is the best day ever," she murmured.

Yes it is. Darnell buried his face in her hair and inhaled.

As they road along the streets, despite the snow falling steadily onto their face, the air sizzled with heat and oozed between them, sliding across his skin like a caress.

Everything feels right, nagged an inner voice in his head. But he kept reminding himself it was just the holiday and what he was feeling was only temporary.

Hours later he was still feeling it as he pulled into his three-car garage. The snow was still coming down steadily and he insisted Liberty and Chance come home with him for one more night. Tomorrow he would take them home and clear away the snow at her house before leaving.

Darnell climbed out the SUV, carried his sleeping son up to his room and laid him across the bed.

"Here's his pajamas," Liberty said as she came into the room. She had already shrugged out of her wool coat and thigh-high leather boots. She took a seat on the full-sized bed beside him and helped pull off his coat and shoes. Chance whined at being disturbed and then started rubbing his eyes as he sat up on the bed.

"Hey Lil' Man, did you have fun today?" Darnell asked.

He nodded and gave a sleepy grin. "Yes." He raised his arms and Darnell slid the shirt over his head, then Liberty pulled the pajamas top on.

"Mr. Dee, are you my daddy?"

Darnell sucked in a long breath then looked over at Liberty. A small smile curled her lips as she looked at him and slowly nodded her head. He dragged in a long breath, then lifted his son onto his lap and looked into his eyes.

"Would you like me to be your daddy?" he asked and noticed his voice was shaking.

With uncertainty, Chance looked over at Liberty. "Can he be my daddy, Mommy?"

Her lower lip trembled as she replied, "Sweetheart, he is your daddy."

His face brightened "Yes! Wait 'til I tell JJ!"

They all shared a laugh and Darnell playfully tickled his belly before helping Chance finish getting dressed and then he hopped in the bed under the covers.

"Goodnight, Chance." He brought his lips to his forehead.

"G'nite," he said, yawning then closed his eyes.

"Goodnight sweetheart." Liberty kissed his cheek and accepted Darnell's hand as he headed to the door. She waited until he pulled the door shut before turning to him.

"How do you feel about that?" she asked.

Darnell drew in another long shaky breath then cradled her to him with one hand at the small of her back. "That was the best Christmas present ever."

"I'm glad," she murmured against his chest.

The energy of the day was still swirling around them like a mini-tornado, holding him captured in the moment with no end in sight.

Not that he was complaining.

He drew back and looked into Liberty's curious eyes. "I want my son to have my last name."

She startled, then her face relaxed as she nodded and said, "I'd like that."

Darnell lowered his head and she released a moan as he kissed her.

♥ ♥ ♥

What is happening? She wondered for the umpteenth time.

She didn't have much time to ponder that thought before Darnell's tongue slipped past her lips with a teasing flick and she felt his heat oozing into her body. *Oh God!* She was melting.

Her arms came around to stroke his back, sculptured arms, and then over his wide shoulders. His kisses were drowning and addictive and she wasn't sure if she could ever get enough.

Darnell deepened the kiss. Liberty felt as if the world was moving and realized he had lifted her off the floor, his hands cupping her ass as he carried her down the hall to the master bedroom. Once there, he slowly lowered her to the floor and her body slid along his thick hard erection.

Quickly they got rid of their clothes and she was back in his arms with his hand cupping her bottom. Her sex throbbed and wept with the need to have him make love to her again. He backed her up three steps and dropped her down onto the bed. She could feel the heat of his eyes as he slipped his knee between her thighs and spread her legs wide.

After several quiet moments, she opened her eyes and met his intense gaze. "What are you doing?"

"Can't I look at you?" he said and his eyes took her in as if he was trying to put everything to memory. "You're gorgeous."

She grinned. "Thank you."

Darnell finally lowered his head and Liberty gasped when his teeth closed around her nipple. It felt so good, she whimpered and shivered. "Dee."

"Did you breastfeed?" he asked as his tongue ran across her aching flesh.

She laughed and shuddered at the question as his tongue swirled around her areola. "Yes, I did." She moaned when he drew her nipple into his mouth and sucked.

"Lucky kid," he growled and then his hand was suddenly down between her legs.

He dipped a finger inside her and tested her wetness, then he brought the slick finger to his lips and tasted. "Mmmm, now I'm the lucky one."

His words and the touch of his hand made her all the more aware of how much trouble she was in. Her breathing increased as his lips and fingers continued to explore and tease. Shivers coursed across her skin.

"You taste delicious," Darnell breathed against her

skin.

A cry ripped from her lips as he closed his teeth softly down on her nipple and made her feel unexplainable things that she was certain she would never feel again.

With a whimper, she realized she was falling in love and it was time for her to bring the magical holiday to an end, but her body throbbed and asked, what's wrong with one more night? And why fight it when she wanted it so much?

Darnell brought his mouth to her other breast, and she felt her pleasure mounting. And in the end, she lost the battle. "Yes," she groaned. "Dee, please make love to me."

♥ ♥ ♥

Darnell loved it when Liberty called him Dee. She only seemed to use it during sex, which was probably why his nickname sounded so erotic and hot, turning him on in ways he couldn't begin to explain. Using his thumb and forefingers, he tweaked her nipples until she nearly came off the bed.

His own breaths were getting ragged. Liberty did things to him... incredible things. He kissed a path down her stomach and felt her belly quiver. How was it possible he had found a woman who turned him on like no other and yet she represented family and forever, two things he didn't want? But there was just something about her that kept him coming back for more.

Darnell kicked the thought out of his head. Nothing was going to spoil this night together. Nothing.

He moved even lower, then draped her legs over his shoulders. "I love the way your pussy taste,"

Darnell explained and then gave a long lick. Liberty cried out as he sucked and licked the sensitive flesh before he pushed his tongue inside.

"Dee!" she cried out and arched off the mattress.

Thrusting his tongue in and out of her, she began whimpering as he increased the pace. And when he brought his thumb to her clit and stroked, Liberty came undone.

"Ooh Dee!"

"That's it babe. Come for me," he coaxed and applied a little more pressure.

Her orgasm came fast and so suddenly she shuddered violently. He continued stroking her with his tongue until the quivering stopped and her hips lowered back onto the bed with a sigh.

"You good?" he asked and she nodded, then sighed.

Thank goodness. His dick was so hard all he could think about was being inside her again. *Would he ever get enough?* he wondered, then shook it off. It was a spell that had to be broken. In the morning she was leaving and he was going back to his quiet bachelor life.

But tonight she was his.

He wasted no time reaching into the nightstand and rolling on a condom then he was between her thighs.

Her heavy-lidded eyes opened. "Horny, are you?"

"Babe, you have no idea how badly I need to be inside you." The overwhelming need was pounding fiercely at his groin. He rolled onto his back taking her with him. She gasped as he lifted her up and onto his waiting cock.

"Awww!" she cried out and clutched at his shoulders.

"Ride me," he growled.

While she rocked her hips, Darnell drew back and then pumped forward filling her again.

Her eyes glazed with lust. "Oh, that's good."

"Just good?"

She moaned. "Okay… it's fabulous… and feels sooo big… and so hard."

Her hair was wild the way he liked it and hunger blazed in her eyes. What was happening between them was better than good. It was almost frightening.

Darnell brought his hands to her hips and thrust upward as hard as he could manage. She was so warm and wet he had to grit his teeth to hold on. Especially when Liberty started winding her hips and squeezing her vaginal walls around his throbbing dick. And finally, he couldn't hold on any longer. The need to explode was so overwhelming he began to buck against her.

"Oooooh," she moaned. "I'm getting ready to come again."

With a sigh of relief, Darnell murmured. "So am I, babe… so am I."

He was beginning to love the sound of her moans and the way her head road to the side.

"Dee," she whimpered.

Her heavy breasts bouncing with each stroke caused him to lose control. He gripped her at the waist and lifted her up and down onto his cock, slamming into her. Her lips parted but no words came out while he kept pumping at a steady hard pace.

"Shit!" Darnell hissed and then he roared and exploded, holding her still until the last wave surged through his body. Chuckling, he wrapped his arms around her and dragged Liberty down on the bed with him. "I'm not done with you so don't even think about leaving this bed tonight." Pausing, he planted a kiss to her cheek. "I plan to wake up with you in my arms."

She sighed and his body eased when she replied, "I think I'd like that too."

Chapter Sixteen

The following morning was one of the most difficult days of her life. Making love and sleeping in Darnell's arms all night had been a mistake. Falling in love with him was an even greater dilemma. And instead of finding closure, her heart yearned for so much more.

Liberty had awakened to him making love to her again. Then they showered and went downstairs and while she made breakfast, Darnell shoveled the driveway and sidewalks. The entire time she was frying bacon, Liberty gazed out the window at him thinking about how wonderful a life together could be, but by the time she started scrambling the eggs, she had given herself a good scolding. As soon as they finished eating she was going home.

The End.

After breakfast, Liberty wiped her mouth and rose as she said, "Thank you, but Chance and I need to be heading home." She had to end it. The sooner the better. Drawn out goodbyes were too hard, too painful.

"Is that what you want?" His amber eyes assessed her from his seat at the table.

No, I want you to ask us to stay.

"Mommy, I wanna go outside and play?" Chance pouted.

Liberty looked over at Darnell with her brow arched.

He put down his fork and nodded. "Sure. Let's go put on our coats."

Liberty decided to join them and a few moments later they all hurried out into the large fenced backyard.

"Let's make a snowman," Darnell suggested and then crouched down, gathered a ball of snow and rolled it in his hand.

"Oh boy!" Chance dashed over to help him. She watched the two of them, and noticed just how patient Darnell was with her son. He was going to make a wonderful father.

He's already a father.

It was true. Any man can make a baby, but only a real man was a father. Darnell had a carefree spirit of a child within himself. It was one of the things about him she admired.

Liberty crouched down and began to ball up fresh snow, joining in on the fun and was happy to see Chance excited about building his first snowman. Why hadn't I thought of it before, she thought with a frown. Probably because she couldn't remember the last time she had made a snowman. Her father rarely had time and she never had many friends to play with. Mostly because during her father's drunken rages, he scared everyone off. *Your life was pathetic,* screamed her inner voice. That was why she did everything possible to make Chance's childhood memorable.

They stacked the snowballs on top of each other until they had a nice round base, then began rolling the second. The snow was starting to come down again and Liberty tilted her head back and caught a snowflake on her tongue. When she lowered her head, she found Darnell staring at her, eyes tinted with desire.

"What?"

"Babe, don't be doing that. I'm thinking of all kinds of things I can do with that tongue," he cooed.

His words caused a slow sizzle. She loved the term of endearment and wished that it could mean so much more, but she wasn't about to be foolish and make more of it than it really was.

By the time they had finished making the snowman the snow was coming down hard. She rushed inside to find a carrot in the refrigerator and used two Cuties oranges for eyes. Standing back they smiled at the lopsided snowman, then she removed the scarf from around her neck and gave it to their frozen friend. Chance was so excited and even though her toes were frozen it had been worth ever second.

They went inside and stripped off their coats and boots and then moved into the kitchen where Darnell made them all a cup of hot cocoa.

Liberty sipped from her mug and stared out the window. "It looks like it's getting bad out."

"I agree. I think you need to stick around at least until the snow stops."

Chance finished his cocoa and lowered from the chair. "Can I watch Lion King? Peeze?"

Liberty spun away from the window and smiled. "Sure, let's go."

Once in the family room, she took a seat on the couch and Chance sat beside her. "C'mon Dad. Sit by my Mommy and me."

Liberty glanced over at Darnell and noticed his shoulders stiffen. A sob clogged her throat as silence filled the room. He took forever to turn around and she knew Chance calling him Dad had ripped straight to his heart.

He finally put the movie in, strode over then took a

seat beside Chance and reached for the remote. She had seen the Disney movie a dozen times, and didn't think she'd ever get tired of seeing it, but today, all she could think about was the three of them watching it together.

Chance leaned back against Darnell's chest, and she smiled. It was amazing how comfortable he had grown.

They felt like a family spending a snowy afternoon together. This was just the way she had dreamed it would be. A husband to curl up with on the couch. A man to share her days and nights. *Oh yes, she had fallen hard.*

Soon the movie ended and the snow stopped. Liberty knew she should leave and head home only she couldn't make herself move. Chance had fallen asleep. She didn't want to disturb him by trying to put on his coat and hat. Besides, he was cranky when he was disturbed. At least that was the excuse she was using.

Liberty who are you trying to convince?

"Let me take him upstairs." Darnell scooped Chance in his arms and carried him upstairs. While he was gone she told herself to get up off the couch and start packing up their things. Only, she couldn't move. Neither could she breathe.

What happened in the next few moments could decide the next path in her life.

Darnell walked back into the room, flipped on football then laid across the couch, dragging her with him. They changed positions so that he was spooned behind her, stroking her side as they watched the game. Liberty's heart was beating so hard, she was afraid to speak and ruin the moment.

He brought his lips to the side of her neck. "I love

having you both here," he confessed.

"Chance doesn't want to leave."

"And what about you?" he asked as his lips closed around her earlobe.

She stifled a groan. "I wish it could always be like this."

"So do I," he murmured. "So do I." His hand caressed her ass and hips and she willed her pulse to slow down. She closed her eyes and enjoyed the magnificent feeling of Darnell lying beside her.

After a while, Darnell's caresses slowed and then stopped. His breathing became soft and steady as he drifted off into a relaxed slumber. Liberty still lay awake as her mind recalled the last few weeks and how much her life had changed in such a short time. And Liberty knew without a doubt, she loved him. How? she had no idea. Maybe it was how patient he was with Chance, or the way he'd stepped up and been a father, or the way he kissed her or even his kind and gentle nature. Whatever it was, it had been enough to make her fall for him.

"What if I loved you?" she whispered, and then she heard his breathing still and his body stiffened.

Darnell wasn't sleep. He'd heard.

And he said nothing.

Oh God! Seconds passed and yet he still hadn't said anything.

Probably because he's been honest with you from the start.

Darnell's arms tightened around her. "Falling in love would complicate things," he said softly. It was probably an attempt to spare her feelings.

Well, it didn't work. She had never been more humiliated in her life.

♥ ♥ ♥

Darnell felt Liberty pull away from him and even though selfishly he wanted her here in his arms, he didn't drag her back. She wasn't really in love. Like him, she was just caught up in the moment. By tomorrow she would have realized how ridiculous the idea was and then she would have a good laugh and it was back to business. Love and committed relationships weren't in his future and she would agree. He loved his life just the way it was. Didn't he? Darnell pushed aside the thought. She would see. He was certain of that. After Chance woke from his nap, he would take them home.

But the thought of them not being here with him caused an ache at the pit of his stomach. The two of them breathed life into the big old empty house. Without them he would be reminded of how lonely the place was and once again wonder why he bought something so big if he never had any intention of filling the house with a family. With that thought in mind, he drew Liberty closer to him, allowing her warmth to ooze his way.

The doorbell chimed through the house. Liberty and Darnell raised to a sitting position, his arm falling from her. *Dammit!* He had forgotten Patrick had planned to swing by to borrow his snow blower. *Talk about bad timing.*

Through the windows, he could see the snow had stopped falling and the sun was shining bright. Liberty stood, and combed a hand through her mass of curls as she shyly looked at him.

Their time together had come to a halt.

Chapter Seventeen

As soon as Cash opened her apartment door, Liberty stepped inside with barely a wave. "Good afternoon to you too."

"Sorry," Liberty mumbled under her breath as she moved straight to the living room and sank onto her favorite overstuffed chair.

"I'm making tea. You want some?" Cash called from inside the kitchen.

"Sure, tea sounds great," Liberty mumbled as she curled into the comfort of the chair and closed her eyes.

Oh God! She had it bad. And only she was to blame.

"I thought Chance was coming with you?"

"No, Sheyna's taking the boys to Beaumont Manor to go sledding."

"Wow! That's good," Cash replied as she padded into the room.

Liberty opened her eyes to see her carrying over two mugs with steam floating on top. "It's hot. Take it," she insisted.

Liberty reached out and took the mug from her and brought it to her lips. "Thanks." Cash knew just how she liked it. One sugar and a squeeze of lemon.

While curling on the loveseat across from her, Cash said, "I'm so glad the family has embraced my little peanut. I bet he loves having cousins."

Liberty nodded and gave her first genuine smile of the day. "Yes, that's all he's been talking about since

Christmas is how many cousins he has. Half of them aren't even his, but all the Beaumont kids are claiming him so he's claiming them."

"Good. That's really good," she said while sipping and Liberty dropped her eyes to her mug under her intense gaze.

"So what's going on with you and Daddy?"

She sighed. "Nothing more than being parents."

Cash gave a rude snort. "Yeah right. I can see it in your face. You're in love with him."

Her head snapped around. "What makes you think that?"

"It's in your voice. Gleaming from your eyes. Come on. Don't try and deny it."

She was right. There was no point in pretending. "Yes, I'm in love with him. Not that it's going to do me any good."

"Why?"

"Because Darnell isn't interested in a committed relationship or marriage," she said and realized she was pouting.

"I'm sure he wasn't interested in having any babies either, but we see how that worked out."

Cash did have a point. "Yes, but we are talking about two different things. With Chance he didn't have a choice, but he does with me."

Cash studied her for a moment. "I don't even have to ask if you've had sex with him again."

Liberty shifted on the chair and tried to keep a straight face. "Yes, I've slept with him."

"I didn't say anything at all about sleeping. I said sex. A brotha that fine I guarantee he knows how to put it down."

"Cash!" she gasped and started laughing.

She shrugged innocently, then took a cautious sip.

"I'm just saying."

Liberty shoved her fingers through her hair and shook her head. "I don't know how I got myself into this mess. I was supposed to just be about me getting to know Chance's father. But then we started talking and laughing and I found out he wasn't trying to steal my baby away, instead he just wanted to be a father to his son, and then…" Her voice trailed off and she sniffed as the first tear fell. "And then he took me out on what wasn't supposed to be a date and the kisses and I started falling for him."

"That's how it usually happens. When you least expect it," Cash said soothingly as she held out a box of tissues.

"Well it definitely hit me like a ton of bricks," she replied and stopped to blow her nose. "Now I'm in love with a man who'll never love me back."

Cash gave her a hopeful smile. "How do you know that? He might fall in love, too."

"Darnell's the type who would fight his feelings to the end."

"Maybe you need to find a way to persuade him," she said and winked.

Liberty immediately shook her head. "I want him to want me for me. Otherwise it would be one big disaster and at the end of the day we still have a son to raise. I don't think I'm willing to lose what we have."

"And what do you have?" she asked between sips. "Amazing sex?"

"We *did* have amazing sex. I refuse to sleep with him anymore."

Cash gave an incredulous look. "*Are you serious*? As long as it took you to find good sex and you want to give that up!."

"Sex complicates things. I discovered that unlike

you I'm an emotional lover. No matter how much I try I can't disconnect my heart from my body."

She shook her head. "Goodness, you do have it bad."

"I know," Liberty said with a sigh and took another sip from her mug.

"You know… things could work out."

Liberty smiled despite how miserable she was feeling. "I'm not going to hold my breath. He and I are at a good place right now. Chance has a family and I don't want to do anything to jeopardize or strain that relationship."

"I don't think you have to worry about that Anyone can see how much he adores that little boy."

She brought the cup to her lips and nodded. "He really does and if that's all I get out of this then so be it." The tears started falling again that she quickly brushed away.

Cash moved over to the end of the loveseat. "I have a feeling everything is going to work out for both of you," she said and reached out to squeeze her hand.

Liberty wished that was true but she wasn't wasting another moment considering that possibility. "Anyway I'm going on and on about my problems. How was your Christmas?" she asked and was glad to have an excuse to change the subject.

"It was a hot mess!" Cash tossed her hands in the air then blew out a long breath. "No one showed up on time, then Mama went on and on about how no one appreciated her cooking anymore, and that the family tradition was over." She paused and gave a playful eye roll. "By the time my sisters arrived, we all hurried into the kitchen, got Christmas dinner on the table and saved the day. It was completely exhausting as always."

Liberty loved hearing her best friend talking about her family. They were the reason why she had yearned for a family of her own. Dysfunctional or not they were still family. That's what she had felt with Darnell and his siblings. A part of something she had no right trying to be included in. Unlike Cash, she had a feeling that things weren't going to end well. And that's what scared her most.

♥ ♥ ♥

Darnell glared at the front door long after it had been slammed shut.

"Dammit," he finally mumbled, scolding himself for being stupid and put the SUV in Drive.

What had he done?

Ever since he told Liberty falling in love with him would be a mistake, their relationship had gone in a different direction. Sure, she still allowed him to see his son as much as he wanted, but the time they had spent sharing him together had ended. The phone calls were no longer dripped with flirtation, and were now brief, straight forward, and to the point. And whenever he invited her to participate on one of his father/son outings, she found some excuse and then declined. And tonight when he brought Chance home, before he could shut off his vehicle and carry him inside, Liberty had appeared on the porch in a sweat suit, boots and a hat on her head. She had hurried across the lawn and took Chance inside despite his protest. In other words, other than Chance, that amazing thing they'd had was now over.

And he missed her like hell.

But what did you expect?

He scowled at the thought as he pulled out of her subdivision and headed down the slippery wet highway toward home. Did he really think they could keep acting like a family in every way possible but the commitment and expect her to continue to be okay with that? Especially when she had already told him in so many words she had strong feelings for him. Was he really that selfish to think he could have things his way?

Yeah, right.

Ever since Liberty had put the brakes on their relationship, he couldn't stop thinking about her. He thought about her when he went to bed and again when he got up in the morning. And every time he thought about their time together on the couch, he wanted to kick himself for his response. If he could go back in time and change the way he had reacted to her confession, he would. Only this was real life and turning back the clock wasn't possible.

He was still thinking about her long after he was in the house and the fireplace was raging. Darnell stepped across the kitchen, opened his large stainless-steel refrigerator and grabbed a water bottle, then moved back toward the family room. He was too agitated to sit, therefore he paced the length of the room while he stared at the Christmas tree still tucked in the corner with the lights twinkling. He wasn't ready yet to part with it or the memories of this one amazing Christmas. It could have been the first of many if he hadn't been such a fool and pushed away the best thing to have ever happened to him.

Now his house was way too quiet. He missed the sound of his son racing through the rooms and his mother's hearty laughter. At one time he had prided himself on his privacy and had customized the house for him. A bachelor pad. A man's cave. Now it was as empty as his chest.

♥ ♥ ♥

Two days later, Darnell decided he was going to lose his mind. Liberty was still avoiding him and he wasn't sure how much longer he could bear being without her. In his bed. His house…, his life was lonely without her. What in the world was he thinking?

With a sigh he closed the case file and leaned back on his chair. Something was going to have to change soon, and he had a feeling that person was going to have to be him.

Before he could ponder the possibility, his phone vibrated in his pocket. It was one of his family members so he dug it out of his pocket, and was actually happy for the distraction. It was Sheyna.

"Hello?"

"Dee, what in the world are you doing?" she shrieked.

He briefly dragged the phone away from his ear and groaned. *Maybe answering wasn't such a good idea.* "What do you mean what am I doing?"

"What's going on with you and Liberty?" she insisted in that sassy tone of hers.

He swallowed the lump of emotion in his throat and rested his elbow on the desk as he replied, "Nothing. We're just friends."

"Friends?" Sheyna gawked. "Friends? Since when?"

A frown creased his brow. "Since I screwed things up. Why?"

"Well then you better fix it quick because Liberty has a date with an optometrist tomorrow night."

Darnell jerked up from the chair to his full height. *"What the hell?* How do you know that?" he barked.

"I was talking to Carolyn Nelson and she said

while she was at the pharmacy she overheard Lee, that's the optometrist, asking Liberty to dinner at Niko's Steakhouse, and apparently she said yes."

As he listened a flash fire started in the pit of his stomach.

"So I called Jamie. She's a manager over at the restaurant, and she confirmed that Lee made reservations for two for eight o'clock New Year's Eve."

Over his dead body.

The rest of her words were swept away on a tide of realization as he paced back and forth across his office. Darnell had to admit, this was one time he was thankful there were so many busybodies in the Sheraton Beach.

"What are you planning to do?" he finally heard her say.

He'd been going through hell for the last week while he tried to pretend as if things would soon be back to normal. But hearing that Liberty was going out with someone else... that she wasn't going to sit around and wait for Darnell to stop running from his feelings was the bucket of cold water over his head he needed. He had been a fool and he'd be damned before he just sat back and allowed another man to claim what was his.

Darnell moaned out loud. "Sis, I fucked up."

"Then you bet—"

"Shey-Shey, trust me," he interrupted. "The only person Liberty will be ringing in the new year with is me."

Chapter Eighteen

L iberty locked up her office and then headed toward the door. She didn't know why she had even bothered to come in. Classes didn't resume until after the holiday season and there had only been a handful of members who had come in to use the gym. Most of them had been in the morning and the rest of the day it was practically empty. By four she decided, there was nothing else that possibly needed to be done and she could manage the front desk herself and had allowed Paula to go home. The college student practically ran out the building.

By the time she had locked up the building at eight, Liberty decided she was the only person in Sheraton Beach without plans on New Year's Eve.

As she pulled into her driveway the snow was coming down again, and prediction was for another two or three inches. Liberty sighed. What a perfect evening. *Too bad I have to bring in the new year alone.*

Cash had a date for the evening. Chance was spending the weekend with Sheyna and JJ. The Beaumonts were having a big New Year's celebration at Brenna and Jabarie's house, and the children were all excited about drinking sparkling grape juice and wearing party hats. She listened with amusement as JJ told Chance about all the fun they'd had last year.

Liberty entered the house and slipped out of her warm boots and coat then slid her feet into the slippers waiting by the door. She strolled into the kitchen for a cup of hot chocolate with marshmallows. While she warmed her tea kettle, she thought about her decision to decline Lee's dinner invitation. At first she thought dinner would have been better than spending the evening alone, but in the end she had called and canceled. She didn't want to mislead Lee into thinking they had a chance. Because he did not.

Her heart belonged to another.

Ever since she'd spent the holiday weekend at Darnell's house, Liberty had been doing everything in her power to keep her distance because if she hadn't she would have run back into his arms and fallen even deeper in love with him.

The kettle whistled and Liberty filled her mug, poured in the dry powder then reached for a spoon and stirred. She always kept a bag of marshmallows in the cabinet for Chance and she tossed as many as she could on top, then moved into the living room and flicked on the television. New York's Times Square was packed with people screaming and laughing, ready to rock through the night until it was time for the ball to drop.

Liberty held out her mug and mumbled, "Happy New Year."

She watched for over an hour, then padded down the hall to the bathroom and was heading back to the comforts of her cozy couch when the doorbell chimed. She hurried to the door and when she looked through the peephole, her breath stalled.

"Lib, let me in so we can talk."

His deep voice caressed her name and caused an unwanted tingle. She had half a mind to send him back out to his SUV, but the other half was hungry to see him and hear what he had to say. She unlocked the door and without a glance, stepped aside so Darnell could enter.

♥ ♥ ♥

"Hey," Darnell murmured, then he kicked the snow off his boots before stepping into the warm toasty house. Without uttering a word, Liberty pushed the door shut then turned and walked back into the living room.

Did you really think this was going to be easy?

Drawing a long breath, he wiggled out of his coat and left it hanging on the front door knob then followed her.

He had gone down to Niko's Steakhouse prepared to confront Liberty and the optometrist, only to discover their reservations had been cancelled. He met Patrick at Spanky's where he tried to talk him out of doing something reckless for almost two hours before Darnell jumped back in his Range Rover and exceeded the speed limit as he drove to her house, his mind racing with possibilities. When he brought his SUV to a halt he had expected to see an unfamiliar car parked in her driveway. And he was relieved to discover there wasn't.

He stepped into the living room to find Liberty was sitting on the couch, the excitement of Times Square muted on the television. With his hands tucked casually inside his front pockets, Darnell stepped further into the room.

"I spoke to Sheyna on the way over. Chance is having a ball," he said trying to ease the tension in the room.

Liberty's face softened at the mention of their son. "Good, I'm glad he's having a good time. He deserves to be happy."

Yes, and so do you. They could all be happy together. "Where's your date?"

He didn't realize he had said it out loud until he saw her eyes widen. "Is that why you're here?" she gawked. "To see if I was with another man?" Liberty sprung from the couch and stormed in his direction. "That's none of your business. Now leave!" Before she could brush past him, Darnell snared her waist, twirling her around and hauling her up against his hard groin.

"Was he here tonight? Did he kiss you?" he demanded.

"What?" Liberty gasped, blinking frantically.

"You're mine," he murmured. "Do you hear me? With her lips slightly parted, Darnell's mouth crashed over hers and touched his tongue to hers. Arousal was a low ache in his body. Reaching up, his hands swept beneath her sweater to cup her breasts, and he heard Liberty groan on contact. She would have to be dead not to feel the sensual charge that sparked in the air. "Mine," he whispered past her lips. And when his fingers grazed across her nipple, Liberty tore her lips free and managed to push hard against his chest, jerking backwards.

"Stop it! I'm not playing house with you anymore," she said while trying to catch her breath.

He didn't know what had gotten into him except that the thought of her with another man made him crazy. "I don't want to play house," he whispered and reached for her arm, but she snatched herself away.

"Then I'm not playing this game!" Tears of frustration pooled in her eyes. "You made your feelings clear so the only thing between us — "

"Lib, could you just sit down and shut up for a moment? Please." He sounded almost desperate but he didn't care.

She inhaled deeply and closed her eyes briefly before she flopped back onto the couch, curling her legs on the cushion beneath her. She still wouldn't look at him.

"Listen, I'm sorry. I had no right to behave like that," he began and then for the longest time he just stood there, staring at her. Her long hair was pulled up into a ponytail. Her knees were bent and she was hugging them to her chest. Even though her eyes were averted his heart jolted. She was beautiful. How could he have been so stupid?

"Liberty this is hard for me. I never wanted any of this and... and then suddenly I find out I'm a father," he began as he paced the length of the room. "But once I saw my son, I knew nothing meant more to me than to be in his life." He hesitated, his gaze shifted to the flickering Christmas tree as he continued. "I planned on being a father without allowing it to change who I thought I was, a confirmed bachelor." He paused long enough to give a strangled laugh. "I'm not gonna lie, in the beginning I had one agenda—charming you with my good looks so I could spend time with my son."

That got her attention. "So you asked me out just so you could get what you wanted."

It wasn't a question and yet he nodded as he looked at her. "In the beginning, yes."

She rose and waved a hand, intending to halt any further explanation. "I'm done with this conversation."

He stepped in front of her, stopping her from leaving the room. "I'm not done, Lib."

"I don't want to hear anymore." Her chest rose and fell rapidly. She dropped her gaze still refusing to look at him, but he brought a hand up under her chin and tilted her head until she had no choice but to look at him, and he saw the anger and the tears lurking in the depths of her eyes.

"There's something about you that I've never found in another woman—and what that was scared the hell out of me. The feelings were so overwhelming, I didn't know what to do except run. But after I heard you had a date with that eye doctor, I realized I was about to lose a piece of my soul."

She scrunched her lips up and frowned. "People really do gossip around here."

"Lib, I love you," he confessed, his nostrils slightly flaring.

"*What*?" She jerked away from his touch. "Dee..."

"Liberty, listen. I know I've said I didn't believe in relationships, but all that changed once I got a chance to know you," he told her, talking fast now before she tried to interrupt again. "With you I have learned so much about life and family ... you and Chance are my family. I need you Liberty. I want you in my life as my wife and the mother of all of my children."

She squeezed her eyes shut and said nothing at all.

"I know you're probably having a hard time believing what I just said and I don't blame you. Hell, I would even have a hard time believing me. But it was you who made me realize I'd rather face my fear of commitment than be without you. I love you Lib. I really do love you." Liberty still continued to be silent and Darnell closed in until her scent engulfed him. He pulled her into his arms and was relieved when she didn't push him away. Staring down into her eyes, he murmured, "Please, marry me."

Liberty finally sighed and threw her arms around him. "Oh Dee!"

He nuzzled a kiss in her hair and exhaled a long breath, breathing in the essence of the woman he had claimed as his.

Hiking her chin up, Darnell seared her with a long penetrating kiss, erasing any doubt in his mind that Liberty was here, in his arms again. And this time he was never letting her go.

He scooped Liberty off her feet and plunked down on the couch with her on his lap. "You scared the hell outta me for a moment there."

Grinning up at him, Liberty fluttered long lashes as she said, "After I heard you say you love me, it took me a moment to find my breath."

Palm to her cheek, he replied, "Well you better get used to it. You'll be hearing me saying those words for a long, long time."

She leaned in closer and purred, "I hope so."

"I love you so much. The thought of you being with another man made me a raving lunatic. I think Patrick was ready to have me committed." His lips tipped in a devilish smirk.

"Is that so?"

He cupped her face between his large hands and nodded. "You are the best thing to ever happen to me." Leaning forward, Darnell brought his lips to her forehead. "These few days without you in my life, I thought I was going to lose my mind."

She nodded and tears filled her eyes as she choked out, "So did I, and I never want to feel like that again."

"Not as long as I'm breathing." He leaned forward, pressing his lips to hers again. "I never want to be without you again."

"You've made me so happy." A big fat tear ran down her cheek.

"And you make me feel ten-feet tall." Darnell ravished her mouth again and again. It didn't matter how many times. It would never be enough.

Abrupt laughter burst from her lips. "I can't wait to tell Chance."

Darnell pulled back and stared deep into her eyes. "Hold up! You never answered my question."

"What question?" she asked and managed to maintain a straight face.

"Ha-ha, quit playing. You know what question," he said. His face softened as he slid out from beneath her and lowered down onto one knee. Liberty rose and he took her slender hand into his. She was staring at him, tears streaming down her face.

"Lib, will you spend the rest of your life with a fool like me?"

One corner of her mouth curled into that beautiful smile that he loved so much. "Yes, I'll marry you."

"Whoo-hoo!" Effortlessly, he swept Liberty into his arms and swung her around in a circle, sending her giggling uncontrollably. She had just made him the happiest man in the state of Delaware. It didn't matter if he'd known her four weeks or four years, nothing would have changed the way he felt about her. If anything, his love would only intensify over time. This was the woman he would love for the rest of his life.

Slowly, he lowered her feet to the floor then Darnell held on to her for another long moment, giving each of them a chance to realize what had just taken place. They were finally together and everything was going to be just as it should be.

"Sweetheart, look." Liberty eased away and pointed to the television. On the screen fireworks were soaring through the air and people were kissing, hugging, and celebrating.

Darnell took the opportunity to kiss her again.

"Happy New Year, Dee," she said a little breathless.

"Happy New Year, Lib."

Epilogue

Darnell stood in front of the wall-length mirror and straightened his tie for the fifth time since he'd arrived. *It's almost time.*

The door opened and Patrick and Dax came bursting in. loud-talking as usual. They were both wearing black tuxedos identical to his. "Bruh, you about ready to do this?" Dax said with a cocky grin.

He nodded. "I've been waiting for this day for almost six months." He caught Dax's expression in the mirror "What?"

His cousin stared at him for a moment longer then scratched his goatee, looking sheepish. "Yo, you sure you wanna do this?"

Patrick chuckled and pointed toward the exit door. "I know, right. Dude, we got the Caddy all gassed up in the back ready to roll."

Darnell grinned. "No way. I'm about to spend my life with the best thing to happen to me. Y'all knuckleheads need to take notes."

"Oh hell no! I want nothing to do with that," Dax muttered, unimpressed.

"Me either. Life is just too sweet for all that." A hint of a wolfish smile lingered on Patrick's lips.

Darnell shook his head again. He had thought the same thing until he met Liberty and now he couldn't imagine a life without her in it.

The last several months had been insane. She and

Chance had moved in with him and her house was on the market. They had grown as a family and he found himself rushing home to be with them. He had already claimed them as his, but today it was going to be official.

The door opened again and his father walked in followed by Chance.

"Hey Dad!" he said and raced over to him.

He reached down and hugged his son. "Hey Lil' Man. You look handsome." Chance gave his signature grin while Darnell straightened his tie.

"Yo, look at little dude. Chance man, you wearing that suit," Dax said.

"He looks just like Dee," Patrick chimed in while Darnell beamed proudly.

His father walked over looking handsome in a dark suit and peach tie as well. Well son," he began and clapped a hand to son, Darnell's shoulder. "You ready?"

He drew a deep breath and met his father's probing eyes. "I'm more than ready."

"Have I told you how proud I am of you? Stepping up and finally being a man."

"And it's about damn time." Scott said and clapped his hands together as he came barging into the room. "Now we need to figure out how to get those two married off." He pointed to his cousins.

Darnell chuckled. "Right. Good luck with that."

♥ ♥ ♥

"Is the bride ready?" Sheyna asked while sticking her head through the door.

Cash looked at her through the mirror and smiled. "Almost. I have to pin up the curls in back and then we're ready to rock and roll."

Liberty looked up from the chair at the two talking as if she weren't in the room. Both of the women looked beautiful in peach dresses.

"Oh your makeup looks so good!" Sheyna squealed.

"Jennifer did it for her," Cash explained as she reached for another bobby pin.

"My daddy's wife is definitely full of surprises," she said with a smile while tucking a strand of dark hair behind her ear.

In the months that she had grown to love the Simmons, Liberty had found the family to be very close and had embraced her as if they had known each other forever.

Cash finally took a step back. "Okay, all done."

"You look beautiful," Sheyna breathed.

And she had to agree.

Liberty released a deep shaky sigh and stared at her reflection. Her hair had been styled in a beautiful upsweep with babies breath and rhinestone combs. For once she hadn't complained when Cash insisted on flat ironing her hair bone-straight for her special day. She rose just as Zanaa came through the door.

"She isn't dressed yet. What have you all been doing?" she scolded and looked at her sister-in-law as she spoke.

Sheyna gave an innocent shrug. "Relax. We had to get her hair and makeup together."

Scott's wife blew out a long sigh, then smiled at the bride-to-be. "You look beautiful, but we have to get you dressed now." She took her hand and ushered Liberty into the other room.

A few minutes later she came out and there was a collective sigh. Liberty spun around. The champagne-colored organza dress was a trumpet design with a high neck decorated in lace and beading.

Cash was grinning and nodding. "Oh, let me get my camera!"

Jennifer returned and was standing with hands propped at her shapely hips and there were tears in her eyes. "Wait until Dee sees you."

Liberty released a shaky breath. *Oh God! I'm about to become Mrs. Simmons.*

The women managed to snap a few photographs before Liberty's stomach clenched and she staggered over to the floral couch and took a seat. "I think I'm going to throw up," she groaned.

Zanaa gasped, "Oh no, not in *that* dress! Hurry! Someone get a trashcan!"

Liberty dropped her head between her thighs.

Jennifer carefully stepped over the cathedral train and lowered on the cushion beside her, holding a small can. "Are you going to be okay?" she asked and placed a comforting hand to her back.

Okay? She was about to get married. She had been waiting six months for this moment, and it was finally here—a July wedding.

"Are you going to be okay?"

Liberty tilted her head and caught a glimpse of Zanaa's worried face. The wedding planner had done everything to try and give her a day she'd never forget so the last thing she wanted to do was worry Scott's wife. "No, I'm fine."

"Just a case of nervous jitters," Sheyna assured her. "I went through that when I married Jace although part of it was because I thought I had to be crazy for marrying his big head." Her words caused infectious laughter to circle the room. "Come on girl. It's time for you to marry my brother."

There was another knock and then Jennifer moved

to the door and returned with her husband.

"Hi," Liberty greeted and admired how handsome Mr. Simmons looked in a black tux with a peach tie and pocket square.

He walked over and dropped a gentle kiss to her cheek. "Young lady, you are definitely a sight for these old eyes."

"Daddy, behave," Sheyna scolded with a playful swat to his arm.

He chuckled. "I'm just saying if she wasn't in love with my son and I was twenty years younger..."

"You would still be too old," Jennifer said and they all laughed.

His eyes simmered with love as he caught his wife around the waist and drew her closer. "Sweetheart, you know my heart belongs to you." They kissed and Liberty felt a wave of longing. *That's going to be Dee and I in about twenty-five years.*

"Alright lady. Let's get this show on the road."

♥ ♥ ♥

The moment the wedding march started, Darnell's heart began pounding and then everyone rose to their feet as the double-doors opened. And out walked his family. Chance was holding his mother's hand guiding Liberty down the aisle toward the altar where Darnell was waiting impatiently for the ceremony to be over so that he and his bride could rush off to spend two weeks in Paris. His gaze roamed across her body, clad in a full-length wedding gown. The dress was lovely, but as far as he was concerned, she could have been wearing a bathrobe and she still would have been breathtaking.

By the time Liberty made it to the altar there wasn't a dry eye in the house. Darnell walked over and stood in front of them, ruffled his son's hair then reached out and took Liberty's warm hands in his. Staring down into her beautiful face, he couldn't help but smile.

"Hey," he said.

"Hi," she answered shyly.

The minister began the ceremony and was asking for the rings when Chance tugged his father on his leg. He paused while Darnell gazed down curiously into his son's round amber eyes and whispered, "Lil Man, what's up?"

"Dad... Can we go to McDonald's? I'm hungry."

Darnell and Liberty shared a look and then exploded with laugher.

Life together was definitely going to be quite interesting.

Fall in love with the families from the beginning...

The Beaumonts
The Second Time Around ~~ Brenna & Jabarie
The Playboy's Proposition ~~ Sheyna & Jace
The Player's Proposal ~~ Danica & Jaden
For You I Do ~~~ Bianca & London
Before I Let You Go ~~ Kelly & Diamere

The Sexy Simmons
The Playboy's Proposition ~~~ Sheyna & Jace
In Her Neighbor's Bed ~~~ Zanaa & Scott

Other Books by Angie Daniels

When It Rains
Love Uncovered
When I First Saw You
In the Company of My Sistahs
Trouble Loves Company
Careful of the Company You Keep
Feinin' (Big Spankable Asses Anthology)
Intimate Intentions
Hart & Soul
Time is of the Essence
A Will to Love
Endless Enchantment
Destiny In Disguise
The Second Time Around
The Playboy's Proposition
The Player's Proposal
For You I Do
Before I Let You Go
In Her Neighbor's Bed
Tease
Show Me
Any Man Will Do
Coming for My Baby
Strutting in Red Stilettos
Running to Love in Pink Stilettos
Say My Name
A Delight Before Christmas
Naughty Before Christmas
Every Second Counts
A Beau for Christmas
Do Me Baby
Time for Pleasure
Seduced into Submission: Curious
Seduced into Submission: Served

About the Author

Angie Daniels is a free spirit who isn't afraid to say what's on her mind or even better, write about it. Since strutting onto the literary scene in five-inch heels, she's been capturing her audience's attention with her wild imagination and love for alpha men. The RT Reviewer's Choice Award winner has written over twenty-five novels for imprints such as BET Arabesque, Harlequin/Kimani Romance and Kensington/Dafina and Kensington/Aphrodisia Books. For more information about upcoming releases, and to connect with Angie, please visit her website at www.angiedaniels.com.